"I think Evelyn Scott is more innocent than she pretends to be," Michael whispered.

"I'm not a virgin, if that's what you mean."

"You don't have to be a virgin to be innocent, Evelyn." His voice was so gentle next to her ear that she could not stop the liquefied warmth that fused through her bloodstream. A series of shock waves reverberated through her body as his tongue plunged into the interior of her mouth and began exploring its depths so thoroughly and lovingly, as if he were seeking some priceless treasure within her being.

Abruptly Evelyn pulled away, startling both Michael and this new, unfamiliar, and reckless self who lived within her body. "No, Michael! I'm not the weak, helpless creature you think I am. Believe me, our war is not over yet. In fact, it hasn't even begun!"

Dear Reader,

It is our pleasure to bring you a new experience in reading that goes beyond category writing. The settings of **Harlequin American Romance** give a sense of place and culture that is uniquely American, and the characters are warm and believable. The stories are of "today" and have been chosen to give variety within the vast scope of romance fiction.

The lush wilderness of Utah plays a major part in developing the executive side of the psyche of Evelyn Scott. She is forced to discover phases of her life she has been afraid to face. In *Untamed Possession* you will realize how the effects of outdoor life can enhance the effectiveness of your business savvy.

From the early days of Harlequin, our primary concern has been to bring you novels of the highest quality. **Harlequin American Romance** is no exception. Enjoy!

Vivian Stephens

Vivian Stephens
Editorial Director
Harlequin American Romance
919 Third Avenue,
New York, N.Y. 10022

Untamed Possession

ANDREA DAVIDSON

Harlequin Books

TORONTO • NEW YORK • LONDON
AMSTERDAM • PARIS • SYDNEY • HAMBURG
STOCKHOLM • ATHENS • TOKYO • MILAN

Dedicated to America's wilderness areas—
"Where man himself is a visitor who does not remain."

———————————◆•◆•◆———————————

Published September 1983

First printing July 1983

ISBN 0-373-16021-6

Books by Andrea Davidson

16—MUSIC IN THE NIGHT
21—UNTAMED POSSESSION

These books may be available at your local bookseller.

For a free catalog listing all titles currently available,
send your name and address to:

HARLEQUIN READER SERVICE
2504 West Southern Avenue, Tempe, AZ 85282
Canadian address: Stratford, Ontario N5A 6W2

Prologue

Evelyn began the silent, rhythmic count in her head. One, two, three, four... the agonizing seconds ticked away, but she knew she only had to endure for a few more seconds, because Roger's kisses had never before kindled a longer, more passionate response. If nothing else, Roger was consistent.

Evelyn's eyes were closed, but that was only because it was easier to think of something else that way. She really did not have time for this. She should be out in the other room with the company president, discussing one of the new South American projects, or mingling with the various vice-presidents and making solicitous inquiries as to the health of their wives and children. Something constructive to her career. There was so much that she needed to accomplish and yet here she was frittering away her valuable time with Roger. Even if she had wanted to—which she did not—she couldn't possibly relax long enough to decide if she liked kissing him or not. There were simply too many more important things to think about.

Five, six, seven, eight.

Roger sighed soulfully. His arms were looped around

Evelyn's waist and her palms were pressed flat against his chest.

"Shouldn't we rejoin the party, Roger?" Evelyn proposed sweetly, knowing that her voice did not sound assertive enough, but hoping that the mere suggestion would be sufficient. She frowned slightly as she remembered the words of her assertiveness training coach when she'd insisted, "Be forceful in your decisions, Evelyn. You're damned lucky to be in the position you're in. Don't ruin it by acting like a woman."

"You don't really care about these corporate affairs any more than I do," Roger scoffed in an alcohol-slurred voice, his arms still clamped around her tightly. "Besides, I've been wanting to have you to myself all evening." He growled seductively next to her ear. "You're much too sexy for your own good, you know."

"Roger, please." Evelyn turned her head to the side, straining her neck to avoid his mouth. "I only came back here to put my purse with my coat. I'm really not interested." There, maybe that was good enough for her coach.

"Of course you are, baby." His clutch around her waist grew more possessive. "Why don't we leave here and go to my—"

As the low, derisive chuckle emanating from a black corner of the dark room reached their ears, they both turned startled faces toward the sound. In his flustered confusion, Roger loosened the grip on Evelyn's waist allowing her to at last free herself from his clutches. Roger glared with open hostility at the man in the corner and Evelyn's speculative expression was a mixture of relief and embarrassment.

"What the hell do you think you're doing in here!" growled Roger.

The man chuckled low in his throat again and stepped from the shadows.

Evelyn's breath was suspended as her eyes tried to focus on the figure emerging from the shadows. Impatient with the darkness, Roger flounced over to the wall switch and flipped on the overhead track lights. The bedroom of their host, located at the opposite end of the house from the party, was now punctuated with white circles, spotlighting Evelyn's dishevelment for this intruder.

Evelyn scowled at Roger. By turning on the lights, he had destroyed any anonymity she might have had. Although she was curious to know who had been lurking in the shadows watching them, she certainly didn't want him to know who she was. All it took were a few screw-ups like this and her well-sculpted career could crumble around her feet.

"Do you get some sort of cheap vicarious thrill watching other people make love?" Evelyn's voice shook as she confronted the large man before her. In an attempt to cover her own embarrassment, she began slowly running her eyes down his frame, critically scrutinizing every detail of his clothing.

Dressed in jeans and a tan sheepskin coat, he was as out of place at this chic cocktail party as a bull in a china shop. But at least he was a stranger. Heaven forbid he should have been someone from the office!

"Making love!" The man's left eyebrow quirked upward. "Is that what you were doing?" he asked in astonishment.

"I think you'd better get out of here," Roger de-

manded with false bravado, his body beginning to
weave from the overindulgence in alcohol.

The man stared indifferently at Roger.

Evelyn looked from one man to the other. Roger's
continental physique did not lend itself to barroom
brawls, and though she couldn't see what was under
the stranger's fleece-lined coat, she could tell from the
harsh shadows that fell across his face that he was used
to dealing with much tougher foes than the likes of
Roger.

"Roger, get me a drink," Evelyn ordered with un-
customary harshness. Roger shifted his surprised gaze
to her. "Please," she added, softening her original
command.

"Look," he began to argue. "I want to get this
straightened—"

"Please, Roger." She had to get these two men away
from each other. How humiliated she would be if, like
a couple of overzealous tavern scrappers, they actually
began to knock each other around.

Breathing heavily, Roger flashed one last warning
glare at the man before leaving the room to get Evelyn's drink.

"Very good," the man said after Roger was gone.
"Have you ever considered becoming an animal train-
er?"

"Very funny," Evelyn's smile was contemptuous as
she brushed her hand primly across her blue silk skirt,
deliberately turning so that the side slit was away from
his view. The skirt revealed a substantial portion of her
thigh and this man might pose problems enough without any encouragement.

The moment that disturbing thought entered her

mind, he took a step toward her. Evelyn stared up at him with wide eyes, and instinct drew her a step backward. "Is voyeurism your trade or is it just a hobby?" Though she tried to appear in control, her voice had an uneasy vibration as she watched him closing in on her like a ruthless soldier advancing toward enemy lines, preparing to lay siege to a new territory.

"Do you want me to show you how it's supposed to be done?" he asked, moving ever closer until his shadow devoured the smaller one Evelyn's body made on the wall behind her.

"What?" she mouthed, pressing her back against his dark, oversized shadow. What possessed her to send Roger away? And what was taking him so long? How could she have been so stupid!

"You seem to be under some misconception about what constitutes making love," he answered calmly, and Evelyn was sure she detected a malicious note of amusement in his voice. "I thought maybe you'd like some clarification on the issue."

"I don't know who you think you are, but..." His hands flattened against the wall on each side of her head, pressing the words back down her throat. She swallowed as his face leaned down toward hers. Her eyes were wide and round, but strangely enough, she felt no fear. Instead, every fiber of her being was aware that here was a man unlike any man she had ever seen. He was totally male in every sense of the word, and incredibly—she frantically searched through her vocabulary for the right word before settling on the term *intimidating*.

"I..." she tried again, but nothing more came forth from her vocal cords.

"Yes?" This time he smiled, and a dimple magically appeared to the right of his mouth. His face was only inches from hers and yet he waited for her to speak.

All rational thought flew out the window at the moment his eyes riveted on her face. Those eyes! They were the most beautiful she had ever seen. Surrounded by thick, brown lashes, they were blue like hers and yet they were markedly different. A darker blue-green color, more like cobalt, they glistened with hidden iridescent elements.

And then she had no thoughts at all. Only sensations. When his lips touched hers, she had expected a merciless assault. But there was only tenderness; a warm, pliable impression that was nothing like the limp, sterile kisses she had endured from Roger and others like him. And despite her original assessment of him, this man obviously didn't have to use brutality to prove anything to anyone. Evelyn was fully aware of the raw power that emanated from deep within him, traveling through the nerve endings of his lips as they gently persuaded her to surrender.

As if it were the most natural thing in the world for her to do, Evelyn's hands had automatically traveled up the thickly cushioned front of his coat, and were beginning to curve over the tops of his shoulders.

"Shall I turn out the lights for you two?" The razor-sharp edge of Roger's voice severed the fragile threads of fantasy that this stranger had been weaving around her. Evelyn pushed at the stranger and pressed her back against the wall, an aura of guilt and embarrassment radiating off her body.

What on earth was the matter with her? Had she lost

her mind? What did she think she was doing kissing two different men within the space of five minutes? Besides, she didn't have time for this. She should be out in the middle of the party, proving to everyone that she radiated success in the social sphere as well as in the business world. After all, she had convinced herself that she had the world by the tail and now her plan was to let everyone else know it.

She looked at Roger and felt a flash of irritation that he would put her in this type of position. She glanced at the stranger. She knew she should feel that same irritation with him, but for some inexplicable reason, it was absent.

"Roger...I'm..."

"Save your breath, Evelyn," he interrupted harshly. "I'm sure you'll be able to cook up a delightful little excuse for your unladylike behavior, but it's really not necessary." He laughed unkindly. "If you think I'm hurt, you couldn't be more wrong. I've only been taking you out because I thought it would give a much needed boost to my career anyway. After all," he said with a smirk, "you are the boss's pet."

Evelyn paled noticeably as Roger spit the cruel taunt at her. But she continued to stand straight, her head held high. She shouldn't be so surprised. These things happened all the time in the business world. Besides, she wasn't looking for any type of deep relationship anyway. A relationship with a man would take too much out of her. She had only so much to give right now and her career was taking it all. Still, it was quite a blow to her ego to learn that there had been no other reason for him to want to date her.

Thinking rationally about it, she had to accept the

truth. She did have a direct line to the company president that few of the other employees had. And this type of manipulative relationship occurred too often in the corporate world for her not to believe Roger now.

She tried to smile stoically.

Still smirking at her, Roger jerked his head in the stranger's direction. "I guess he's just that extra little bit of added insurance, right?"

Evelyn glanced at the stranger in confusion. Before she could ask Roger what on earth he meant by that remark, he slammed her drink on the small bedside table and stepped back into the hall, closing the door behind him.

Evelyn held herself straight as a ramrod, raising her chin and blinking rapidly. She was not going to cry. She wasn't. There was a time and place for everything, and this definitely was not the time or the place to cry. She would get out of this situation with the same aplomb she always had for sticky predicaments.

She caught her reflection in the mirror over the dresser and shuddered. Her skirt was drastically misaligned and her matching silk blouse looked like she had slept in it. What would everyone think! She had always been the epitome of fashion and style. Thank heavens this man who was seeing her in this less than perfect state was not connected with her company! But what a cold, unfeeling person he seemed to be.

"Thank you for standing up for me," she snapped irritably at the stranger leaning casually against the wall. "I hope you enjoyed my humiliation."

"You should have defended yourself." He shrugged.

Again the words of her assertiveness training coach threaded through her thoughts. "Don't ever expect a man to stand up for you. You must be the one who remains in control. Only you."

"You're quite right," Evelyn answered haughtily as she looked into the mirror and ran her fingers through her hair, readjusting the gold comb behind her ear. "I'm quite capable of looking out for myself."

The man smiled as if he found her statement amusing, and Evelyn stopped primping for a couple of seconds to stare at him in the mirror. Had she said something funny? She did not recall that she had. Mentally shrugging, she checked to see if her lipstick had been smeared too much by the two very different kisses. Look at him, anyway. Dressed like some dumb Montana rancher who has come to the big city for the first time.

"You're not from around here are you?" she smiled condescendingly at him as she surveyed herself in the mirror.

"I live in Utah."

"Utah," she repeated dully. "How nice." Utah, Montana, what's the difference. A backwoodsman is a backwoodsman. "Well, if you'll excuse me, I have work to do." With one last glance in the mirror, she headed for the door.

"Work?" he asked. "I thought this was a party."

Evelyn's hand was on the doorknob, but she stopped and turned to stare at the man as if he were some sort of prehistoric troglodyte. "Is your occupation in the area of physical labor, Mr.—?"

"Baylor," he smiled that same amused smile. "And, yes, I work outdoors."

"Ah, well, Mr. Baylor," she smiled with her same condescension. "That explains it. You see, I'm sure that to someone in your field, a party is a party. Mugs of beer after work at the local tavern, no doubt. But to me, a party is simply a continuation of the workday. So now if you will excuse me..." She opened the door and stepped out into the hallway.

Through the door behind her, she heard a low chuckle that vibrated along every nerve ending in her body, a disquieting sound that for some strange reason, struck a fearful chord deep within the secret reaches of her soul—a place she never wished to visit.

Straightening her shoulders once again, she forced her mouth into a smile and walked directly toward one of the company vice-presidents.

It was two hours later before she could leave without anyone thinking it an impropriety. She had managed to make her presence known to each of the corporate leaders and was satisfied that she had proven just how versatile Evelyn Scott could be.

After collecting her cream-colored mink and silver evening clutch, she thanked her host and began reciting her polite good-byes. She was aware, as she had been for two hours, that the big bucolic peasant from Utah was watching her. She had thought he was preparing to leave two hours ago, but after she'd left the bedroom, he had removed his coat and rejoined the party also.

Now, as she left the apartment, he actually seemed to be following her. A momentary bud of apprehension sprouted in her mind, before it was quickly uprooted by common sense. Without a doubt, he was a backwoods nuisance, but an actual menace? She doubted that seriously.

She had thought about approaching Roger for a ride

home, but he'd already found another female companion to occupy his attention. Well, she decided, she would simply take a taxi. That would certainly pose no problem.

"How are you going to get home?" The man was directly behind her as she walked down the front steps of the apartment building.

Evelyn turned and smiled in fake surprise, as if she were only just now seeing him. "Oh, hello again. I'm taking a cab."

"You came with Lover Boy, didn't you?"

Evelyn spun around furiously. "I really don't think it's any concern of yours whatsoever, Mr. Baylor," she answered icily. "I am quite capable of getting myself a taxi and finding my way home."

He quirked his eyebrow in disbelief, infuriating her even further.

She raised her hand to hail a taxi and noticed, out of the corner of her eye, that he too was signaling for one.

"Shall I get one for you?" he asked politely.

"No, thank you," she answered curtly. "I'm quite capable of hailing my own."

"So you said," he smiled mockingly.

As one pulled along the curb, she opened her purse to make sure she had enough change. She didn't like flashing large bills to anyone late at night. She rummaged through the small evening bag, her fingers becoming more and more frantic as she searched in vain for her wallet. She stopped. Oh, no, she must have left it in her other purse at home! Knowing she was coming to the party with Roger, she hadn't been that concerned about having money with her. And now she had nothing. But how was she going to get home?

The taxi driver was drumming his fingers impatiently against the steering wheel, and when Evelyn slowly shook her head to indicate that his services were no longer needed, he sped off into the night looking for another fare.

She turned and saw the stranger from Utah standing on the curb, his arm draped across the open back door of a cab. He was watching her with self-assured smugness, his head cocked fractionally to the side.

"Problems?" he asked, knowing damn well that there were problems.

Evelyn ignored him and glanced back up at the building from which she had just come. She nibbled worriedly on her lower lip while trying to decide what on earth she was going to do. She really couldn't go back in and ask one of the officers of her company to lend her the money. It would appear as though she couldn't even handle her own finances. Nor would Roger be the one to ask. She looked into the gaping darkness of the empty street, realizing that it would be terribly unwise to walk. And she didn't even have the money for a bus! How could she have allowed herself to get into this situation?

She turned to the man who, only moments before, she was cursing as a provincial hayseed. "I—I don't suppose you could loan me some money for a cab. I seem to have left my wallet at home." Oh, how she hated to have to ask this rustic oaf for anything.

"No," he answered bluntly, then smiled at her startled face with infuriating ease. "But you can share my taxi with me." He swept his hand expansively toward the backseat, motioning for her to enter.

Sighing heavily in defeat, Evelyn walked over to the

cab. She raised her chin, staring defiantly at the man for one long second, then scooted into the backseat of the car.

"What would you have done if I hadn't been here?" he asked after she had given her address to the driver and they were on their way.

She resented the question and her expression said as much. But the truth of the matter was she didn't know what she would have done. Even if she had told the driver to wait at her house while she went in to get the money, there was always the chance she wouldn't have had enough cash in her other purse. "I would have figured out something," she lied easily.

He began to laugh softly again. "You never give up, do you?"

She turned a bewildered face toward him. "I'm afraid I don't know what you mean."

"I was watching you in there tonight, trying to figure out what it is that drives you so hard. If you're bucking for the presidency of the company, I hate to inform you but I think the position is filled."

"I am not bucking, as you so crudely put it, for anything, Mr. Baylor," she ground between clenched teeth. "You obviously do not understand the intricacies involved in working for a large corporation."

"Oh, I understand all right. But I certainly didn't see any of the men there working as hard as you were."

She laughed at his ignorance. "I don't know in what century you live, Mr. Baylor, but in this day and age a woman in business must work twice as hard as a man to achieve equal amounts of success."

"Does that mean you can't take time off to enjoy yourself at a party the way the men there were doing?"

Evelyn looked out the window at the passing neon signs and the man was watching the alternate play of shadows and light flicker across her face, wondering, yet already knowing, what it was that pushed this woman to such extremes.

"My life is scheduled differently than a man's," she answered somberly.

He stared at her, his features drawn and disapproving. "Leaving no room for play, in other words."

She looked at him for a long moment, searching that sturdy face that reflected the wide-open frontier. A man like that could never understand. His work was the physical kind. He was a man who lived by different, simpler rules. He lived where life obviously was dealt with on a different plane. The code of the West, she concluded narrow-mindedly.

She tried to smile, but the expression was empty of emotion. "That's right, Mr. Baylor, no play."

When the taxi stopped in front of her building, Evelyn stepped out onto the curb. "There's really no need for you to walk me to my door. I'm really quite capable of—"

"Do you realize that's the third or fourth time you've said that to me?" He gave the driver a hand signal to wait.

"Said what?"

"That you are quite capable." They reached the top of the stoop and he gently grasped her arm above the elbow, shattering in a touch the icy wall she was trying to erect against him. "Are you really afraid to let the world know that Evelyn Scott might have just a teeny-tiny weakness or two?"

"How did you know my name?"

He laughed again. "I thought that was the idea tonight. To let everyone at the party know who you were. And to convince everyone that Evelyn Scott is a hard charger."

"You make me sound like a bull," she frowned.

He watched her carefully, responding without words. There was no need for a verbal response, for his eyes said it all.

Evelyn looked away from him, trying to pretend he was just like any other man, but the attempt did not meet with much success. There was an almost imperceptible wisp of sadness in her voice as she spoke softly.

"I'm on a treadmill, Mr. Baylor. A treadmill that cannot be stopped." She looked at his face for signs of comprehension before continuing. "I know you cannot possibly understand what I'm saying to you, but my explanation will have to suffice. You see, I do not have weaknesses. There simply isn't room for them in my life."

She was unaware of the exact moment when his lips closed over hers. All she felt was a rhythmic sway inside of her. And then a feeling that she was falling into the quiet abyss of space. For the first time she could remember in her life, her body and soul were completely in the hands of another. Evelyn was not in control.

She had no idea how long he kissed her. All she was aware of was the end of the lovely, helpless feeling. She stared into his concerned face as he held her at arm's length.

"Don't try to be Superwoman all of the time, Evelyn.'' He smiled sadly. ''Step off of the treadmill once in a while.''

Long after she closed the door to her apartment and the stranger had disappeared into the night, Evelyn saw his strong, open face and heard the caressing stroke of his voice.

''It's a good thing you do not live around here, Mr. Baylor,'' she quietly spoke the words aloud. ''I most definitely do not have room in my life for you.''

Tonight she felt burdened even more than normal by this ever-increasing weight that seemed to press down upon her life. She had found only one form of release for such pent-up pressure, and though it alleviated the problem only temporarily, it was all she had. So, following her daily pattern, Evelyn Scott sat on the couch and allowed the tears to flow freely.

Chapter One

As she sat in the hard-backed chair with seven other presumably unsuspecting victims from around the country and listened to the director of Expanding Horizons, a double-edged blade of anxiety shredded the already strained nerves inside Evelyn's stomach. How could her boss have done this to her? To think she had naively believed that Lloyd looked upon her as a daughter figure! And he had aided her career through so many crises before. But what sane man would send a daughter he cared about to a place like this?

It had only been a month since he first mentioned that laughably ridiculous term, "executive enrichment," and then informed her that it was either "participate or no promotion." Oh, he had not said it in precisely those words, but his meaning was blatantly clear to the three Antron executives he had singled out for this "enriching" experiment.

Long ago, Evelyn had learned some basic tricks for succeeding in the corporate world. She'd eventually wedged herself into a position of confidence with her boss by appearing to listen with rapt attention to his frequent rambling conversations.

Knowing it couldn't hurt her career, Evelyn had always feigned interest in Lloyd's superlatives over the noble deeds his godson had performed. Though the "child" had served in Vietnam and was now a lawyer or something equally magnanimous, her boss still felt compelled to proudly list the little fellow's each and every achievement. What he never realized was that while Evelyn sat before him with a look of complete absorption her thoughts were actually on the continuous stream of paperwork, leases, legal or ecological hangups that made up her workday.

But did all those hours of sitting in Lloyd's office while he rattled on about little Johnny or Mikey, or whatever the heck his name was, help her in this instance? Oh, no! Nothing she said would change his mind about this wilderness experience for corporate executives. She tried everything to get out of it, from pleas to threats to childish tantrums.

On that fateful day, Lloyd had paced his office, hands in the pockets of his vested wool suit, his voice quivering with lofty self-importance. "If your body is dead, then your brain too will eventually die. By mastering the physical challenges offered by Expanding Horizons, this wilderness experience will help you gain greater confidence in your job responsibilities and will probably give you more emotional security in your personal life.

"Think of it as a summer camp, Evelyn," he had said. What she'd wanted to tell him was that she had no earthly idea what a summer camp was like. She had never even been a Girl Scout, for God's sake. She hated the outdoors!

Now here she was, two thousand miles away from

her plush New York City apartment, in the wastelands of Utah, listening to the director of Expanding Horizons using frighteningly unfamiliar terms like "rappelling," "carbiners," "ropes course," and "flea's leap."

She couldn't make it. She could not survive!

"Let me make one thing clear at the start," the director of the school addressed the group of seven. "This is not a summer camp."

Well, well, Lloyd. Strike one for you.

"Some of you are here because you've been here before," the director continued. "Most of you realize that you need physical as well as mental challenges in your life. Some of you are here because you are being groomed for promotions and your companies feel that this will prepare you for greater responsibilities in your profession. This program, like that operated by Colorado's Outward Bound, was developed with officebound executives in mind. We have found that isolation is widespread among corporate executives. Here, at Expanding Horizons, there is no chain of command. Everyone interacts and shares in all of the raw experiences with each other."

Evelyn fidgeted uncomfortably in her hard-backed chair and began nervously examining her fingernails. She did not have time for this. Seven whole days! There was no room in her life schedule for seven days in the wilderness!

Had it really been only three hours since she and her two co-workers, John and Frank, disembarked from the plane at Salt Lake City's airport? It seemed so long ago, a lifetime away....

Whisked from the airport in an antiquated military jeep, the three executives had been given a brief tour of the surprisingly modern city as they drove toward Immigration Canyon.

Viewed from downtown Salt Lake, the Wasatch Mountains rose like a wall of granite before them, a time-scarred battlement that quickly swallowed them whole as the jeep began its steep climb through the narrow canyon. The cool wind whipped Evelyn's raven hair into complete disarray and she constantly struggled to keep it in place.

"Don't worry about your hair." John Stimmer smiled, looking at Evelyn in a different, more intimate way. "You look beautiful with it that way."

"Yes, Evelyn dear, we've never seen you when you weren't the absolute picture of perfection," Frank Groden added snidely.

Ignoring Frank's undercurrent of hostility, Evelyn became absorbed in the surroundings. As the road slanted upward, sage bushes and juniper trees quickly gave way to aspen, pine, and blue spruce.

"Where are the chrome and glass buildings, the factories, the ticky-tacky suburbia?" Evelyn could hardly control her surprise at seeing nothing but trees, and wild flowers, and lichen-covered rocks, and space. Open and free.

"It's startling to realize that there is actually land left in this country that's not inhabited," John reflected.

"Shouldn't it serve some purpose?" Evelyn questioned innocently.

Frank turned around from the front seat and sneered at her. "That's just typical of your closed-mindedness,

Evelyn. What's wrong with it serving no purpose other than to exist in its natural state?''

Evelyn declined comment. She and Frank had never gotten along and their departments were constantly at odds with each other. But their problems had magnified two months ago, when Frank tried to initiate a closer, more romantic, alliance with Evelyn. Forcefully rejecting his bumbling attempts had caused a deeper rift in their already shaky relationship.

But she was not going to think about Frank. This trip was going to be taxing enough without dwelling on animosities around the office. Instead she had tried to think over what he'd said about land existing in its natural state.

It should have been a reassuring thought, but instead the untrodden landscape filled her with an almost overwhelming sense of isolation, of forbidding terror. She was an outsider who did not belong here. The farthest west she had ever been was Kansas City and it had seemed as remote and culturally deprived as another planet to her. No, she did not belong here. This was not a friendly territory. It did not want her and she could not survive.

As her mind reeled with the awesome possibilities of terror that awaited her, their driver had continued to steer the jeep through the curving canyon, finally turning onto a rutted dirt road. Gearing the transmission into four-wheel drive, the truck pounded along the path, low-lying branches brushing against the passengers' sides.

Dirt clogged Evelyn's pores and her eyes were filled with dust. With each rotation of the wheels, she felt as if her spine were being jammed upward into the base of her skull. The driver gripped the wheel tightly to keep the vehicle in line, and all conversation ceased as teeth clattered and bones jarred. After what seemed an eternity, the truck had finally come to a halt in front of a large log-framed lodge surrounded by several smaller log cabins.

Evelyn wearily lifted her body out of the jeep and, once standing on solid ground, brushed at her skirt and pale yellow silk blouse to remove the dust and grit.

For the last half hour, all she had been able to think about was getting to her room and having a nice, hot, leisurely soak in the tub to wash away the dirt and grime from that irksome jeep ride. She was thankful she'd had the foresight to bring her bath oils. By the looks of this place, she would be lucky if they even provided soap.

After the luggage was unloaded from the truck and unceremoniously deposited inside the front door of the lodge, the three executives were offered cups of coffee that tasted as though it had been made several days ago, then were introduced to the other three men and one woman who would be a part of their group.

The interior of the lodge was rustic. A large stone fireplace covered the far wall and the only furniture in the room consisted of two large easy chairs, a worn, brown leather couch that sagged in the middle, and several hard wooden chairs. An old oak table along one wall held the large coffeepot and a balanced arrangement of assorted stale pastries. On the walls were topographical maps and charts depicting the various species and classes of flora and fauna in the area. From her chair, Evelyn could see through an open doorway, where uniform rows of wooden tables comprised the dining room. How, she wondered, could they be expected to stay in such a dreary place?

"We've had much success with our program over the years." The director's voice echoed in the almost hollow room, pulling Evelyn's thoughts back into the harsh reality of the present moment. "And I hope that you will all be satisfied with what you learn about nature and about yourselves."

A ride through Central Park in a taxi was as close as Evelyn had ever come, or desired to come, to nature, and she wasn't at all sure she wanted to know about any deep, dark secrets that lurked within herself.

Besides, this was not part of her life plan. She had to reach perfection, yes. And she had to prove to everyone how valuable she could be. But this! A seven-day trek through the wilderness was not on her career agenda. As it was, it took every hour of every day to cram in all of her obligations. Seven days away from the office could spell doom for her position!

"Now, I'll get out of the way and turn you over to your instructor for the expedition. Michael? You want to come in here?"

Turning in their seats, the seven guests stared with unconcealed curiosity at the man entering the lodge. The one who was to guide them into the unknown, who would become master over their fates, the man they would have to trust with their lives and their sanity.

Grabbing a doughnut and taking a bite of the pastry as he passed the table, he walked over to the mixed circle of willing and unwilling participants.

Evelyn's breath suddenly caught in her clogged throat. Something inside of her began to beat wildly. She blinked. She was shocked and yet she was curiously remote and numb as she watched the man moving closer.

Chewing the last bits of stale Danish without haste, he winked at Evelyn and, nodding to the others, swallowed, and pulled a chair over in front of the group.

"I'm Michael Baylor and I'll be the leader in your brigade." He turned the chair backward, straddled it and leaned his weight on his muscular arms across the wooden back.

Evelyn held her breath, waiting for the wood of the chair to splinter and crack under the dominant strength of the man occupying it. Some part of her brain was appalled while another sector calmly accepted the absurdity of this situation. Too calmly.

As his eyes swept the group, they landed on her. He smiled crookedly, and she realized with full force that the image of his face had never really left her mind. Though her life had few unfettered niches where a man could settle, this big outdoorsman from Utah had somehow managed to squeeze uninvited into an existing space and lodge.

His cobalt-blue eyes were the same as she remembered from that night two months ago in New York. Here they shone brilliantly in the fading half-light from the windows, like an incandescent flame that flickered and softened the austerity of the room. Yet all she would allow herself to remember about them was the way his penetrating stare had taunted her determination and ambition, ridiculed her desperate need to succeed.

He was undoubtedly the most magnificent looking man she had ever seen. She knew that when she first saw him at that cocktail party in New York. But at the same time, it was a frightening kind of appeal he held for her, one to which she was not at all accustomed. He was nothing like the men she knew and dated in New York. His presence forced her mind to conjure up fanciful pictures of a different place, a different time. Days of old, when sturdy frontiersmen conquered and tamed a land that was as savage and unrestrainable as they. Or when hale and hardy adventurers were lured away from the security of their homes and deep into the wombs of mountains by golden visions of the mother lode.

Michael was a tall man, at least six feet three. And though his weight was probably at a minimum for his height, his powerful muscular structure gave him an imposing advantage over the other men in the room.

"I hope to get to know all of you on a personal level before this expedition is over." He smiled. "But for now, why don't each of you introduce yourselves and tell us something of what you do for a living."

Was it Evelyn's imagination or did his eyes seem to linger a little too long on her?

How could this be? It wasn't that small a world. Besides, she was two thousand miles away from the spot where she had first met him. She had been on the verge of accepting this strange turn of events as quite a coincidence, but was it? After all, he was at the company party that night. Was he there for the purpose of drumming up business for this school? Perhaps he had been at the party to pick over the employees as if they were seasoned peaches, choosing which ones were ripe for this course in primitive survival.

Evelyn's mouth was growing tighter by the moment. So that was why he had followed her around all night. For the last two months, she had tried to erase the indelible furrow he had carved that night into her narrow, wooden existence and she had convinced herself that he had been nothing more than a lovesick puppy who latched onto her at the party. But now his presence there took on a new significance. She slowly shook her head in angry disbelief as the realization sunk in that on that night he actually had been a bloodhound, pursuing juicy rabbits for the sacrificial feast.

He was the one who must have convinced Lloyd that this program was perfect for his executives. He was the one who was destroying the neatly laid guidelines she had set up for herself. He was the one who was stealing seven precious days of her life.

She had never really liked the man, and now she knew why. He was trying to change her life. And she had no intention of letting him get away with it. She would "do her time" if she must, but when she left this godforsaken place, she would be the same woman she had been before she came here. In control. On top of the world. The epitome of the successful woman of the eighties.

As if he could read her thoughts, he glanced sharply at her, causing a strange shiver of apprehension to follow the course of her spine.

"You first." Michael's voice and gaze, both commanding and sharp, were riveted on Evelyn.

She noticed his eyes evaluating her silk blouse and brown linen skirt with that same condescending attitude he'd had that night in New York. As his gaze took in her skillfully applied makeup and long black hair, repaired from the jeep ride and now sleeked back into a precise chignon, she caught a quick flicker of disdain before it was masked over with professional objectivity.

Michael was trying to figure out what it was about this woman that intrigued him so. It had been that way since he met her two months ago in New York. He knew the minute he met her that his program was imperative for her. She was too much of what he himself had once been. Nothing was as important as her career. There was no time to enjoy life on a simpler basis. He knew this wilderness course was for her.

And yet, it was more than that. Despite her cold attitude toward him that night in New York, he had been unable to forget the feel of her body in his arms. He remembered the way she had given herself up to his kiss, letting go of that obsessive hold on ambition and success. Though only for a few brief moments, she did relinquish all control to him.

If only she would do that again; trust him enough to relax her guard for a little while. But, at the rate she was going, it looked like it was going to be an uphill battle all the way.

Evelyn continued to fume inwardly. She didn't know anything about other women who might have been through this course. All she knew was that she—Evelyn Scott—was a lady. And there was no way she would let Michael Baylor or anyone else turn her into some untamed mountain barbarian.

Reluctantly she stood. "I'm Evelyn Scott." Her voice was a monotone that reflected her obvious scorn for this entire meeting. "I'm manager of the land department for Antron Oil, and I am here for this—this—"

"Adventure?" Michael smiled.

"Program...because my boss"—the word was issued as a snarling expletive—"who was obviously sold a bill of goods about this place, insisted that I come. It is the only reason I am here, and I want it understood from the outset that I am here under duress and that if anything happens to me, this school and Antron will be held responsible.'' Clamping her mouth closed tightly, she sat down, carefully making sure the pleats of her skirt were not buckled underneath her.

Michael rested his forehead on his arms briefly, trying desperately to hide his laughter. When he had finally brought all but a few chuckles under control, he lifted his head and spoke to the others in the group. "Evelyn is our resident hard-charger. She's competing for *Time* magazine's Man of the Year award. Next?" He pointed to John.

Evelyn's face froze at the not so subtle put-down of her personality. Irritation pressed her lips into a thin line, and in retaliation for his criticism of her, she set her pale blue eyes to the most enjoyable task of mentally picking him to pieces.

Ignoring the fact that his body looked to be in perfect shape—a fact she had taken note of that night two months ago—she concentrated on his apparent lack of style in dress. His camouflage pants, jungle boots, and drab green military-style T-shirt made him look more like a misplaced Green Beret than an instructor in a two-hundred-dollar-a-day wilderness school.

His hair was thick and darker brown than she had remembered, and much longer than the short cut so many New York executives were sporting these days. In the back, it hung just barely over the collar of his shirt and in front, slight waves defied any semblance of style. I'll bet he cuts it himself, she thought callously, angry at herself for having to resort to such catty thoughts. But it was his fault. She was a respectable woman in business and was normally above that type of behavior, but this man made it impossible for her to think like a professional.

Michael glanced up sharply, catching her cool appraisal of him, and as a further irritant to her, she saw that he was amused. Weblike lines fanned out from the corner of each eye, making small indentations in his tanned skin as his gaze narrowed on her in humorous speculation.

Pointedly turning his attention away from her, he then listened as each member introduced himself. Evelyn only listened with half her attention, caring nothing about their lives other than where they worked. Her life was now in too much of a shambles to care about anyone else's.

"What about you, Michael?" Charles Stipple, the executive from IBM, asked and all attention, including Evelyn's, riveted on their instructor.

"Okay, that's fair," he smiled with infuriating confidence. "I was a ski instructor at Alta for three years and was on the Utah Ski Patrol. I was a Special Forces' paratrooper in Vietnam..."

"Green Beret?" Walter Green, the boy scout leader from Wichita, Kansas interjected.

"No, but I worked closely with some of them. Why, were you one?"

"No." Charles puffed out his chest slightly. "I was Army, fifty-fourth division out of Inchon. But of course my playing field was Korea."

God! Evelyn grimaced. Why did men always have to wallow in all that military hogwash? They—meaning all men—were like overgrown kids, trying to recapture their lost youth and some mysteriously vague machismo. And at the same time, they constantly needed to be coddled and pampered by women.

"Anyway," Michael continued, "I've been working for Expanding Horizons for the last two years. Are there any more questions? Yes, Dorothy?" He turned his attention to the participant from Arkansas.

Dorothy Miller, the only other woman in the group, stood. She was somewhere in her mid-forties, large, buxom, and rough cut from her bone structure to her complexion. She was wearing a denim jacket and faded jeans over her muscular legs. Her hair was short and looked as if it had been hacked off haphazardly with a pair of dull scissors.

"Like I told ya'll a while ago, I've been through the program twice before and both times under you, Michael." Her gaze widened to encompass all the members of the group. "He's a great leader and knows everything there is to know about the wilderness. If I didn't think so, I wouldn't have come back for my third course." Finishing her endorsement of Michael's ability and of the course, she plopped heavily back into her chair.

Evelyn grimaced. Her third time! Why did the only other woman in the group have to be one who looked like she could hold her own in a scrimmage with the Pittsburgh Steelers?

"Thanks for the vote of confidence, Dorothy." Michael smiled at her with a familiarity that, for some inexplicable reason, made Evelyn immediately dislike the woman.

"Okay," Michael cleared his throat. "If there are no more questions, I think we should talk about what we're doing here ... that is, all of us except Miss Scott, of course, who is here under duress."

He smiled wickedly at Evelyn and, in return, she glared at him with a look that could kill. She would get even. Some way, somehow, she would make him pay.

He began to recite:

"Two roads diverged in a wood, And I
—I took the one less traveled by,
and that has made all the difference."

Awkward silence hovered over the group, each with his own private assessment of their leader's sanity.

"Does anyone know who wrote that?" Michael asked.

Oh, great, a lesson in literature! Evelyn groaned inwardly, trying to conjure up a feeling of superiority over this overgrown, backwoods boy scout.

"Frost," the man from Boulder, Colorado spoke up. He was a professor of sociology at the University. Totally bald and with a paunch around his middle that prevented even the slightest waist bend, Evelyn wondered how on earth he was going to make it through a supposedly rigid physical program like this one.

"That's right," Michael smiled, revealing a dimple on the right side of his mouth that was both appealing and disconcerting to Evelyn. She had noticed it in New York and it had stuck in her mind as one of those irksome details that would not go away. It didn't fit him. A man that large and rugged and intimidating should not have a dimple! "Robert Frost," he said. "And the name of the poem is 'The Road Not Taken.'"

"I quoted from it because that is exactly what we are going to do. We're going to take the road less traveled by and I hope—I'm confident—that it will make all the difference in the world in your lives. You will never be the same again. Certainly, you will all—" He glanced swiftly at Evelyn, as if setting her apart from the others. "Most of you will jump back onto the treadmill that is your life in the big city and the memory of these seven days will fade somewhat. But, believe me, you will never forget this experience. You will either be enriched by it or... or it will defeat you. The outcome is entirely up to you."

"Isn't that your job?" Where did that sarcastic question come from? Evelyn didn't recall forming it in her mind or on her tongue. Suddenly, everyone in the group was staring at her, and she noticed the slight smile that formed on one side of Michael's mouth, a smile that was also a half-laugh.

"Isn't what my job?"

"To make sure we're not defeated."

"My job, Evelyn"—the way he spoke her name sounded as soft and resonant as silver—"is to make sure that the equipment the school supplies is in good working order, that you know how to use it, and that you don't get lost from the rest of the group. You aren't planning on gaily tripping off into the woods by yourself are you, my dear?"

She didn't answer, knowing that to fence with this man would be an exercise in futility. Simply being around him was enough of a drain on her energy. What little she had left should be reserved for pursuing a legitimate way to get out of this program.

"You should all realize that I won't be holding your

hand through this. You must do it on your own." Once again, he was directing his attention to the whole group. But his last words, "holding your hand," planted a seed deep within a dark sphere of Evelyn's mind. Suddenly a thought, a wonderful, awful idea slowly began to germinate.

Could she really get away with it? She had never done anything this outrageous in her life. She had gotten where she was in life with intelligence and an overwhelming drive to succeed.

Her looks had certainly not been a determining factor. If anything, they had hindered her climb up the corporate ladder. Very few men believed that a woman as attractive as she was could also have a mind as competent as hers.

But something had to be done to free her of this situation. And Michael Baylor did not seem like the type of person with whom she could reason. She had to do it. There was no other way. Mustering up the courage to go through with this brash plan, Evelyn Scott smiled. It was the first time she had done so all day, and it was a most unpleasant smile.

"Okay." Michael stood and set his chair aside, hoping that everyone understood completely that they were on their own. No way was he going to play nursemaid to these people any more than he ever had to the members of his groups. "Let's talk now about specifics of the course. Come over here." He walked over to the table and began haphazardly stacking the doughnuts and pushing them to the corner by the coffeepot. After brushing any crumbs onto the floor with his palm, he lifted a paper cylinder from the floor and began unrolling it on the table.

The large map he unfolded was colored in shades of green and brown, the darker colors representing the more primitive regions of the mountain range. Circles and squares and triangles dominated the center, and dotted red lines fanned out in several directions.

Everyone was leaning over the table, trying unsuccessfully to decipher the meaning behind all those dots and lines and squares.

"This area of the mountains is called the High Unitas Primitive Area. That is where we'll be doing most of our training. Here is the lodge." He pointed to the largest black square. "Four miles over here is the first campsite. Tonight is the only night you'll be sleeping at Base Camp. The rest of the nights will be spent in sleeping bags."

Groans over the future accommodations rumbled through the group.

"Right here in this clearing is the ropes course. That's where you'll learn the commando crawl, jumping from rock to rock, inching along a rope strung fifteen feet above the ground, and"—he smiled with devilish glee—"the tramway ride."

"What's that?" several voices asked in unison.

"I'll let that be a surprise." There was another round of groans from the group and Evelyn became more and more irritated by Michael's sadistic brand of humor. Didn't he know, didn't he realize how terrified they all were?

Her eyes darted nervously from one member of the group to another, trying to gauge their fear in relation to her own. John Stimmer had always been able to retain a poker face, so his expression was as calm and collected as always. Frank, on the other hand, was drumming his fingers nervously on the table and licking his thick lips continuously.

Charles Stipple, the executive from IBM, and Bill Adler, the sociology professor, watched Michael intently, as if removing him from their sight for only a minute would spell their certain doom. Walter Green, the boy scout leader from Wichita, Kansas, looked as eager and excited as a preschooler to begin this new adventure. And Dorothy Miller, to Evelyn's further agitation, stood there nodding her head with approval over Michael's chosen route, her face filled with supreme confidence in herself.

"I'd like to strangle that incompetent idiot who sent us here," John muttered under his breath.

"Amen," chuckled Evelyn, who was standing beside him.

"What was that, John? Evelyn?" Michael raised his head from the map, and feigned a look of interest in their conversation.

"They said they'd like to strangle our boss, Lloyd Sullivan, for sending us here." Frank laughed, more at the thought of embarrassing John and Evelyn than over the remark itself.

"Incompetent idiot, I believe you referred to him." Michael leaned against the wall and folded his arms across his chest, as if waiting to hear more.

"That's right—idiot!" Evelyn's fear exploded into shards of bitter resentment. "He sends us off to the boondocks with absolutely no idea what is waiting here for us."

"You mean he's never been here." Michael frowned, as if he were trying to get all the facts straight in his mind.

Evelyn huffed impatiently. "Of course not," she

snapped, her tone relegating Michael to the same idiot status as her boss. "The closest Lloyd has ever come to a wilderness adventure is when the air-conditioning conks out in his Winnebago."

"No," John added playfully. "I think you're wrong there, Evelyn. I distinctly remember hearing that Lloyd stayed once in a hotel without valet parking."

"All right, everyone," Michael smiled tolerantly and tried to bring order back among the now slaphappy group. "Enough of that." He cleared his throat and continued, "In this direction is where we'll do most of our rappeling and climbing."

Oh, God! Evelyn prayed silently, fear once again her primary emotion. *This does not fit into my life plan, at all.*

Michael's voice droned on. "On the fifth day, you will rest... alone. Each of you will experience twenty-four hours of solitude in the mountains, after which you will be required to find your own way back here to Base. It will probably take you a day or a day and a half to make it back."

"Alone?" Evelyn's pulse began to flutter with an indefinable kind of fear and her stomach curled into tight knots of dread. Surely he didn't expect her—Evelyn Scott, who absolutely and unequivocally abhorred the outdoors—to do all those things! There was no way she could rappel and climb and leap and be alone in the woods—and still live.

"That's right, Evelyn... alone."

The feeling that she was soon to lose control of her life seeped through the pores of her flesh and clung to her vitals. No! She had to remain in control. She had built her life on control. What was it her assertiveness coach said? Keep telling yourself over and over that you are responsible for your own life. You are in control. Yes, she must remember that.

The tiny seed that had been planted by Michael's remark a few minutes earlier was beginning to take root. She would have to plan her strategy very carefully. Her performance would have to be supreme.

She looked at Michael for a long, searching moment, wondering whether he was the type who would fall for it. More to the point, she wondered whether she would be able to play that kind of role. She had convinced herself for so long that she was a winner, that she couldn't lose. This was her chance to prove it.

For if Evelyn Scott did, in truth, have the world by the tail, then Michael Baylor should be nothing more than a bothersome flea bite with which to contend.

Chapter Two

Oblivious of the calculated workings of Evelyn's mind, Michael leaned back over the table and continued outlining the schedule for the next seven days. "Tomorrow morning, we'll meet at four o'clock out front and—" At the clearly audible gasp, Michael's eyes jumped from the map to Evelyn's face, and shifting his weight from his hands resting on the table to the wall beside him, he expelled a long sigh. "Is there something wrong, Evelyn?"

His casual stance against the wall and the upward tilt of one dark eyebrow convinced Evelyn that he wasn't really as angry as his voice intimated. Again, he seemed almost amused.

"No...No...I just...isn't that a little early?"

"Too early for you, love?" She jumped at his casual use of the endearment. "What time would you like to get up? Perhaps we could bring you your breakfast in bed."

Oh, what a despicable man he was! Making fun of her in front of the others that way. He thought he had the ultimate control over her because, by some devious means, he had tricked Lloyd into sending her here. Well, he had another think coming. Hadn't she shown him in New York that she was capable of holding her own against him? He may have gotten her here, but she would make him very sorry he ever thought that she would cower under his dominance and power. "Four o'clock is just fine, Mr. Baylor," she snapped.

"Good, now shall we continue?" He paused momentarily, his dark gaze narrowing as he watched the sympathetic look and touch that John Stimmer bestowed on Evelyn.

Was there something between the two of them? he wondered. She didn't seem the type to become involved in an office affair. But one never knew. He tried to suppress the irrational dislike he suddenly felt for John Stimmer, and cleared his throat and forced his attention back on the agenda.

"We will work as a team, but each of you"—he paused and glanced sharply at Evelyn—"is expected to pull your fair share."

"How many miles will we hike each day?" Charles asked.

"It will vary, depending on the terrain and your stamina. I like to play that sort of thing by ear."

"What if one of us gets hurt?" Bill's voice carried a slight nervous quiver.

"If it's a minor injury, we'll take care of it out in the field. If it's major, I carry a walkie-talkie so that we can get help."

"What if...?"

"How will we...?"

"When do we...?"

Evelyn was only vaguely aware of the questions and

answers that floated around her. Fear and her brash plan to obliterate that fear consumed her conscious mind.

Evelyn was snapped out of her semi-trance when Michael finally finished answering all of the questions and rolled the map back into a tight cylinder. "What you're going to do now is learn how to fill your packs and roll your bedding." He led them over by the cold fireplace where seven nylon backpacks and sleeping bags were piled on the floor.

Though she tried not to be, Evelyn was mesmerized by Michael's demonstration. His hands, his movements, his voice all flowed together in perfect harmony, a blending of humor and eloquence and skill. She tried to shake the hypnotic spell he had cast upon her, but every time he looked in her direction, all independent thought vanished.

Michael noticed that Evelyn was now paying close attention to every detail. Maybe she had decided to cooperate after all.

"Now"—he smiled, reassured that she was going to cause no further problems—"the packs, when loaded, should weigh no more than forty pounds. I have a list here of the things you should put in your pack tonight. Follow the list carefully, because I don't want anyone complaining about his load being too heavy to carry."

Too heavy to carry! The realization hit Evelyn's conscious mind like a stick of dynamite. They were expected to carry their own packs? "You mean we... have to carry these... things on our backs!" Her voice was higher pitched than normal.

"Evelyn. Evelyn." Michael puffed out his cheeks and blew air through pursed lips. He walked over to her and put his hands on her shoulders, sending a dangerous current of electricity through her nervous system. Her gaze jumped to his face, where his blue eyes narrowed and drilled into her with an intensity that was frightening. But his mouth was smiling. Again, it was wrong. The eyes didn't fit the mouth. Was he irritated and perturbed at her or was he amused? She hated this helpless feeling of being trapped on a one-way street, as if he could read her thoughts but she could not read his.

Michael wanted to be angry, he really did. But there was something so vulnerable about her, so childlike and innocent, that he could only feel amused. A somewhat cynical amusement, he decided, but amusement all the same.

"Who did you think was going to carry your pack?" He was shaking his head slowly in amazement.

"I—I don't know," she answered naively. *Why can't I make myself tell you to get your big, warm hands off of me?* "I just thought you would have ... someone ..."

"Lackeys maybe?"

"Of course not!" She jerked her body away from his touch, but it took a conscious effort to keep the rising hysteria out of her voice.

"There's no need to be so hard on her." John Stimmer rushed to her defense, ignoring the cold stare Michael was sending his way. "Evelyn's not used to—to—"

"To what?" Michael's impatience was beginning to show.

"To reality," Frank drawled sarcastically.

"To rude men, for one," Evelyn retorted, encompassing both Michael and Frank with her remark.

"Oh." Michael cocked his head and pouted. "Was I rude to you, Evelyn? I'm sorry."

Like hell you are, she thought, too angry to find a proper comeback. Why did she let that man upset her so? Even that one night in New York—on her own turf— he had manipulated her emotions until she wasn't even sure of her own well-calculated direction in life.

"But let's get one thing straight from the beginning." His tone was no longer one of false contriteness. "I am not a social director. This is not a Sunday afternoon picnic in the park. This is a wilderness survival school. In my eyes, you are all the same. There is no distinction between male and female, between strong and weak. You are simply students, without gender and without specific privileges. Is that understood?"

Everyone, except Evelyn, nodded.

"Evelyn, I didn't see your reaction. Is that understood?"

"Perfectly." She ground the word between clenched teeth, trying very hard not to tell this big buffoon what he could do with his special privileges.

"Okay." He expelled another heavy sigh. "Now let me show you how to roll these sleeping bags. Walter, would you volunteer to help with this demonstration?..."

After more than an hour, the group had practiced rolling and unrolling their bedding and stuffing and restuffing their packs at least fifteen times.

Evelyn watched Michael closely. She knew that if she were to carry her plan through to victory, she would have to convince him that she was attracted to him. But was she? She had asked herself that too many times since that night in New York and she had never come up with a satisfactory answer.

He was much too masculine, too rugged to be called handsome. Handsome was a term reserved for men who had a sense of style, of grace; men who were softer, more manageable than this giant of a mountain man. She had known from the first moment she laid eyes on him that he really wasn't her type at all. He was simply too intimidating.

She was relieved when, after final words of advice and instruction to his charges, Michael suggested that they all turn in for the night.

"As Evelyn noted, it's going to be a very early start in the morning." Michael again winked at Evelyn, filling her with unwarranted anger. "The cabins have two beds each," he continued. "So I suggest you decide who you're going to bunk with for the night. You two women will share the first cabin. And, Evelyn, you'd better cut those fingernails, because they won't last beyond noon tomorrow."

Her chin jutted out sharply. She was way beyond the point of letting people tell her what to do. Who did Michael Baylor think he was anyway? She looked down at her perfectly formed and polished nails, the ones she had just had manicured at the salon only two days ago. Cut them? It was unthinkable!

"I think I can worry about my own fingernails, Mr. Baylor." She was seething with some unexplainable anger toward him. She tried to analyze it, but couldn't understand the reason. It was a combination of so many things; her uncontrollable feelings of attraction for him, his ability to have her transported from civilization to this godforsaken wilderness, his attempts to gain control of her life, his perverted plan to convert her into some sort of mountain goat, her own lingering fears of being manipulated, her lack of confidence... her loneliness.

"Suit yourself," he muttered.

Be ruthless, Evelyn. Be ruthless! "I always do," she lied smugly.

At that bold assertion, his eyes riveted on her for one long, agonizing moment that seemed to consume all of time and yet, in reality, only lasted a few seconds. But in those seconds, his careful gaze traveled with seductive leisure over the length of her body. The other members of the group were shut off from them. They seemed to exist in a space of their own. Evelyn's breath caught in a lump in her throat and her heart began to pound erratically as she felt the heat from those intense blue eyes moving slowly, inch by infinitesimal inch, across the firm angles of her face and the pliably soft contours of her body.

He couldn't decide exactly what it was about that woman that continually set his teeth on edge. He couldn't even make up his mind if he wanted to enfold her in his arms or knock her around a bit. Just looking at her made his blood run warm with both lust and annoyance.

Evelyn watched entranced as he ravaged her with his blatantly sexual stare, and she tried to force a feeling of revulsion into her thoughts, tried to find the strength to deny him this access to her being. But somewhere in her mind the signal got crossed and only the liquid fire from his eyes poured into the circuitry of her bloodstream.

She had said that she always suited herself, but that

was not true. Right now, she was not suiting herself at all. She was once again allowing this man to manhandle her well-trained emotions.

Without her awareness, her face had hardened with the mental reminder to retain at least a front of dominance. But when the last threat of Michael's patience was shredded and he finally responded to her smug assertion that she always suited herself, the threat, though barely above a whisper, seemed to penetrate her flesh and reverberate like waves throughout her body.

"Not anymore." There was not a trace of a smile on his lips or in his eyes.

The cabin that the two women were to share was nothing more than a nine-foot-by-nine-foot box with a set of crudely built bunk beds, one irregular and filmy window, a gray metal sink, and a black, potbelly stove. There wasn't even a bathroom! Evelyn scowled as she realized that she could forget the idea of a leisurely soak in the bathtub.

"This used to be a logging camp," Dorothy explained when she noticed Evelyn's expression of dismay. "The cabins were used strictly for short stays." In one fluid movement, Dorothy swung her bag onto the top bunk and, using her hands on the mattress for support, lofted herself onto the upper bed.

As dismayed over Dorothy's physical prowess as over the accommodations, Evelyn sighed and dropped her makeup bag on the lower bunk. The two larger bags were left directly inside the entrance to the cabin. It had taken every ounce of strength in her body to manage the three pieces of luggage as far as she had. Her mouth automatically hardened as she remembered Michael's cynical expression when he noticed her matching pieces of blue luggage a few minutes ago on the lodge porch.

"May I ask why you brought two large suitcases and one small one for a seven-day wilderness expedition?" His laughing tone had been an obvious mask for his scorn.

"Because I do not care to look like a refugee from some war." She had stared pointedly at his own attire, and to her disappointment the action did nothing more than to serve his warped sense of humor.

"But, Evelyn"—his mouth curved into that sadistically wicked grin of his—"I thought you knew—this *is* a war."

"What is a war?" she asked haughtily, her patience rapidly shredding to nonexistence.

"This...adventure." She did not like the way he said that word. "For you it will be a war against nature. You will be battling forces that are far more awesome than any you would face in a military confrontation. Believe me, I've seen both. When I'm finished with you, you will feel like a refugee from a war." There was a subtle change in the look of his eyes, one she could not even begin to understand.

"So what's your point?" She tried to insolently remove the uneasiness he caused in her. "That I should go ahead and accept defeat by dressing like you do?"

He made a great show of looking down at his clothes as if he were seeing them for the first time. Brushing away an invisible speck of dust from his shirt, he smiled flippantly, proving that her barb had not hurt his feelings in the least.

"Wear what you like, Evelyn. All I'm suggesting is

that you accept here and now that you cannot control the circumstances that will affect your life in the next seven days."

Now, alone with Dorothy in this dismal cabin, Evelyn shook her head to remove the nagging suspicion that Michael had been referring to something more than the survival course. It was as if he knew her thoughts, knew of her plans.... No, that was absurd! She shook her head again, but the feeling remained. It was going to be a war, that much she could guess. But with whom? Or what?

Mentally exhausted, she eased her body onto the lower bunk bed only to find herself atop a mattress that was so hard it could have served as an exterior wall for the cabin.

"I think I've made a big mistake." The statement was directed to no one, but Dorothy immediately pounced on it.

"What do you mean?" She leaned over the edge of her bunk and stared upside down between her dangling legs at Evelyn.

"How bad is it going to be?" Evelyn lay with the back of one hand pressed against her closed eyes.

"The course? Hell, girl, it's no big deal. Look." Dorothy sprang down from the upper bunk and leaned against her arms tucked under the upper mattress. "Did you see some of those men in our brigade? Shoot, my ten-year-old daughter could outmaneuver most of those yellow-bellied sap suckers. The idea is to show them you're as tough as they are. Those male chauvinist pigs are expecting us to drop dead by noon tomorrow. But we'll show them, won't we? We'll show them what we women can do...."

Dear Lord! Not only was she roped into this horrid experiment in the boondocks of Utah and then verbally assaulted time and time again by their uncivilized instructor, but she had to bunk with a die-hard feminist from Arkansas! Even so, she didn't have the heart to tell this relatively harmless woman that she had no intention of competing with the men in this program. Her only intention was to get through it as physically unscathed as possible.

"That's why I come here every year," Dorothy continued now that she was on a roll with a captive audience. "Every summer I get to show up a different crop of men."

"Are you married?"

"Sure am. Been married for twenty-five years to the same man."

"What does he think? I mean about you coming out here to—to show up men?"

Dorothy looked puzzled for a long moment. "I don't rightly know. He did say once that it sure made it easier living with me the rest of the year. I guess I work off all my steam and frustrations when I'm here. Yeah, I guess that's it. It'll sure work off your frustrations."

It'll sure work off your frustrations. Lying on the rock-hard bunk in the dark, Evelyn listened with growing discontent to the rhythmic sound of Dorothy's breathing. If only she could relax like that and sleep.

Why did it seem that all of her life was a battle? Other people talked of being laid-back, taking it easy, letting things ride—terms and clichés that had no relevance whatsoever to Evelyn's existence. She had never once let anything ride, and she could certainly not be labeled as laid-back.

Since she was thirteen, her life had been geared toward one thing—success. Physical work, her aunt used to say, is obsolete. Don't fall into the trap your mother is in, she would harp. Make something of yourself. Make yourself so valuable that no one would dare leave you.

Evelyn knew that's what it all boiled down to in the end. A way to insure that she was never left out in the cold the way her mother had been.

Her father's mid-life crisis had left its scars on all of them. Evelyn was only thirteen and at a too impressionable, too naive stage when her father deserted them. It was his selfish pursuit of happiness at the expense of everyone else—from the affair with his twenty-two-year-old secretary to his escape to see the world through the eyes of Club Med—that began to drive the hard edge of life into Evelyn's realm of awareness.

But even more than the loss of her father, it was the realization of what little control her mother had over her own life and her daughter's. Her mother's education was limited, therefore her skills were too, but it was her lack of drive that kept them from attaining financial and emotional security.

All the while, Evelyn observed and digested and dreamed. One day, she swore to herself, she would be in the position where no one could ever force her into the dire straits her mother had been in.

· It had been one long battle after another to make it as far as she had in her career. In the beginning, she had not had the confidence to carry herself continually upward. But with the help of assertiveness training and the involuntary toughening that comes with a heart that is wounded so early in life, she had created a life for herself that revolved around one thing and one thing only—success.

She worked sixty hours a week trying to make herself so valuable that she would never be left defenseless as her mother had been. A hard-charger, Michael called her. If she was, so be it. It was too late to change what Evelyn Scott was. She had been raised on a battlefield, and now that she was thirty-one, the end of the war was still nowhere in sight.

Even now, she had this new skirmish brewing on the front lines. She would have to enter a new battlefield and fight to regain an upper hand. But she could do it. Evelyn was accustomed to winning. Her life goals had been centered around victory and so far, she had tasted little defeat.

Except that, this time, her opponent was more formidable than any others she had faced. Was it just his rugged masculine dominance that depleted every reservoir of strength in her body? Or was it the way he looked at her, the way he seemed to capture her very essence with his eyes, as if she were a wounded doe caught in the paralyzing, hungry stare of a stalking mountain lion?

Angry at herself for allowing this inner weakness to bubble to the surface, she threw the army blanket back and slipped quietly off the bunk. After pulling her midnight blue, velour caftan on over her head, she ran her hand over the soft material and glared disdainfully at the meager contents inside the backpack in the corner of the room.

Dorothy, naturally, had stuffed her pack in about fifteen minutes, while Evelyn had fretted and stewed for an hour over which clothes to take. Damn Michael Baylor! She had bought so many nice, new outfits for the trip, but now because of his stupid army boot-camp agenda, most of the things she brought seemed grossly inappropriate. However, if she had limited herself to just those items on the list, she would have had nothing to carry. It was ridiculous to expect a woman like her, who had always been on everyone's best-dressed register, to comply with that bare-bones list. If the pack was too heavy to suit Michael, he could just carry it himself.

Sighing over the chic, but now wasted, wardrobe that was to be left behind, she walked to the door of the cabin and slid the metal bolt lock to the side. As noiselessly as possibly, she opened the door and stepped onto the cabin's small plank porch.

To ward off the chill, she crossed her arms, holding the caftan against her body. She slowly breathed in the pure, cold night air before pulling a slim cigarette from her pocket and lighting it. The pine trees, silhouetted against the night sky, appeared black, and the rising mountains loomed ominous and dark all around the campground. The smells and sounds were so different from the ones she was used to hearing. Where were the blaring horns? The barking dogs? The constant stream of canned laughter on the television, or conversations on the radio, or in the apartment next door, or on the sidewalk below? Only the sound of the wind whispering forlornly through the pine trees and the occasional shrill night song of a bird fell upon her ears.

It was disconcerting, this quiet was. She was sure she could never get used to it. The noise of the city left little room for self-reflection. But here, with this absolute stillness, one could easily be haunted by his or her own conscience, nagged by those fleeting doubts that attacked one's sense of direction. No, she didn't think she liked it here at all. It was disrupting her life in a devastating way. In a fit of irritability, she ground out her half-smoked cigarette on the railing of the porch.

Scanning the layout of the base camp, Evelyn noticed a small, orange ember that glowed and flared occasionally in the direction of the lodge. Squinting her eyes, she peered into the dark to try to locate the source of the glow. She stepped off the porch onto the cool, brown dirt of the packed trails between the cabins and headed toward the tiny, glowing light.

She was within ten feet of the lodge porch when she realized her mistake.

"Looking for me, love?" A velvet-smooth voice stroked the night. She froze in her tracks as her eyes adjusted to the darkness and she focused on the man on the porch. Even if she had not seen the face, she would have known the voice. On that night two months ago, it had ingrained itself upon her mind, its inflections and tones a part of her memory and her future.

Michael was leaning back in a wooden chair, the bottoms of his boots propped against the railing. A cigarette was held tightly between the tips of his thumb and fingers. A flick of his little finger sent the excess ashes spinning off into the air.

She frowned at his self-assured presumption. No, she tried to convince herself; she wasn't looking for him. She wanted to avoid him as much as possible. And yet, if she were to get out of this ridiculous regimen of torture, she would have to do something.

She had decided earlier in the evening that this was the only way. But now that she was here, face to face with him, she was afraid to commit herself to this course of action. It wasn't her style at all. She had gotten where she was in the business world on skill and drive alone. She knew women who used their feminine wiles to get what they wanted and she had always abhorred such tactics. Now here she was considering the same moves for herself. But there was no other way.

Breathing deeply and straightening her spine, she climbed up the three steps to the porch. "Did you know I was a candidate for this program when you were in New York?" She kept her mouth tight and her eyes hard.

"Not until after I met you," he answered calmly.

"I see. Was there something about my personality that made you think I should come here?"

"Everything about you made me think you should come here."

She had been staring at the space on the floor under his legs, but her head snapped up at his last statement. "In other words, you knew that I couldn't spare the time for this, so you decided to demonstrate your power over people by making sure that I had to come here. Is that correct?"

"That's not correct at all, Evelyn."

"Then what? What possible reason could you have had for suggesting that I come here."

"Sit down. You're cold," he said, startling her with his direct order. Crushing out his cigarette, he dropped his feet to the floor in invitation for her to sit at the now vacant spot on the rail. She reluctantly settled herself on the wide railing only to have her feet immedi-

ately clasped in his hands and placed on his lap. He
began rubbing against the tops of her feet with the
palms of his hands.

"Don't walk around without shoes here. The air is
deceiving. Because it's so dry, it doesn't feel as cold as
it really is."

His words went right over her head. All she absorbed
was the sensation of his two work-roughened hands
massaging the soft flesh of her feet.

As Michael's hands touched her skin, he marveled at
the pale softness of her arches, the slim toes capped
with red polish, ankles that tapered upward into long,
slender legs.

Evelyn felt a weakness sweeping throughout her
body, pulling all strength and fight out of her. She
wanted to stop this onslaught of sensations, wanted
desperately to retain her superior position. But before
she could force her body to react and pull her feet back
into the private folds of her robe, a man walked out the
front door of the lodge and stopped beside them.

"Ah-ha. So this is the one." A red-headed man with
a full beard leaned down and smiled as he peered in-
quisitively at Evelyn. "I'm Josh Winslow."

Startled by the sudden intrusion of reality into this
fanciful world of sensations, Evelyn could only nod.
She tried to make some sense out of his remark, but
failed miserably. What did he mean when he said "So
this is the one"? Had Michael Baylor already spread
some unsavory jokes about her around the camp?

She snatched her feet away from his hands, wrapping
the robe more tightly around her ankles. Well, she didn't
have to stand for that. She had never before tolerated
that kind of ungentlemanly behavior. But then . . . what

was her alternative? If she didn't follow through with her plan, she had nothing to look forward to but seven long and arduous days and nights of physical torture. She shivered again as she glanced furtively at Michael. She wasn't at all sure if she could fake attraction for this man or not.

"Evelyn's tongue is as frozen as her feet I'm afraid," Michael grinned, breaking through the awkward silence that had hovered around the three people on the porch.

If nothing more than to prove that he was wrong, Evelyn calmly held out her hand to Josh. "I'm Evelyn," she said affecting a seductive slur. Without regard for the sudden hardening around Michael's mouth, Evelyn cocked her head provocatively to one side, purring, "Are you going to be with our brigade, Josh?"

Clearing his throat, Josh laughed awkwardly. "I hadn't planned on it, but..."

"Get lost, Winslow." Michael's deep voice cut the air with sharp incisiveness. Evelyn's gaze jerked to Michael's face and was confronted by his intense glare.

"Yeah...well, I was just going. Good luck, Bale-out!" Josh glanced with amusement at Evelyn and then back to Michael. "Looks like you're going to need it." With an index finger salute, he was gone.

After watching Josh walk away, Evelyn kept her head turned to the side, presenting to Michael a vulnerable, but deliberately hard, profile.

"What are you thinking about?" he asked, wondering why in the hell he even gave a damn. He had been sitting here thinking about her for the last hour, trying to figure out why this beautiful woman was so afraid to let down her guard with anyone, and also wondering why he should even care.

Her eyes darted about in nervous agitation as she searched for a plausible lie. "I was curious about the name he called you. Bale-out?"

"Being a paratrooper in Nam, it was the likely choice for my nickname. Josh and I were in the same platoon, stationed outside Saigon." He watched her closely for a minute. "But that's not what you were thinking about, Evelyn. Why don't you tell me why you can't spare seven days out of your life for this?" he asked, his voice low and soft in the still night air.

Evelyn kept her head turned to avoid looking at him. His presence was too overpowering. "It isn't simply seven days. It's a lifetime. I have a job that does not stop just because I'm not there. The world keeps on turning...turning without me, I might add."

"And you're afraid you'll be left behind?"

"I'm not afraid of anything." She clenched her jaw tightly to keep the lie from escaping to the surface. "But I'm a very goal-oriented person, and this seven-day hike through the woods does not move me one step closer to my goals."

"Instead of moaning about the fact that you've been dragooned," he advised, "why don't you think of this as an opening to new possibilities? Let yourself be unstructured for a while. Coast a little bit. Surely after all the years you've been working, you deserve it." His head was cocked slightly to the side, his mouth pulled into a soft smile.

Coast...coast. That was the word he used. And that was, of course, what she had in mind. She was not thinking of the same thing he was, but still—he did say it. But would she be able to convince him to let her do just that?

"Coast, yes, you're right," she purred, noticing his sudden frown out of the corner of her eye.

He was silently tense for a long moment, knowing that she had shifted this conversation to another area entirely, but not yet sure to what level. She looked very touchable in her dark blue robe, soft and feminine. She stirred something within him and he wasn't about to stop and analyze why or how.

Standing up to stretch his long legs and torso, Michael took a couple of steps toward her, forcing her to sit back against the railing. Placing his hands on the rail to each side of her, he leaned close. The cabins were bathed in the light from the full moon above, while the porch itself remained in shadow. His face was very close and Evelyn realized that, even in the shadows, she was seeing too much man for comfort. Breathing deeply to still her rapid heartbeat, she tried to adopt a seductive pose.

"It must get awfully lonely up here for a man...like you." She forced herself to look at him and the suddenly hard expression that looked back at her as if it were chiseled from stone almost made her back down.

Michael's mind went blank for a moment, before the significance of her statement sunk in. He felt a burning anger that competed with the rapidly billowing desire he had for her. What kind of stunt was she trying to pull? He knew she wasn't happy about being here, but how far would she actually go to get out of this wilderness experience?

Michael lifted one hand to the shoulder of her robe, where he began to finger the soft velour fabric. His gaze followed the movement of his fingers for a moment then lifted back to her face. "Sometimes" was his quiet reply. "Why?"

"Well," she swallowed, wishing now that she had never ventured into these waters, knowing that it could be more treacherous than she had intended, and yet also knowing that she could not now swim safely back to shore. "I was just thinking that maybe we...you and I...could make some sort of deal."

"Deal?"

"Yes. A bargain." Since he hadn't immediately shut her off, her confidence was returning. She could not go through with this physical torture. Ever since that day, at the age of thirteen, when her aunt told her that physical work was obsolete, she had avoided any kind of physical activity. She had built up her skills in social and intellectual areas, learning how to dress and cook with a flair, voraciously devouring the technical and educational components needed to become a success, and perfecting the savoir-faire that it took to be a choice executive. Those challenges she could handle. But this?

"What kind of a bargain?" She was staring at his broad chest expanding and contracting under his T-shirt and she missed the hard glint that touched his eyes. His hand moved back to the railing.

"Well, I was sent here under duress."

"As you've made perfectly clear," he muttered.

"Yes...well, this...this wilderness stuff isn't exactly my cup of tea." She chanced a glance at his face and now saw two eyes that flickered with amusement. She gritted her teeth and continued. "I don't particularly want my body to get...hurt in any way."

"Why? Is your body used in your line of work?"

Breathing in sharply, she glared at him. How dare he! "How dare you! As you well know, I happen to be a land man for one of the country's largest oil companies."

"Really." He sounded disinterested. "Don't you mean a land person?"

"The title is *land man*. I have no problems with people mistaking me for a man."

"You're sure of that?"

This was taking the wrong turn all of a sudden. She had to get back to her original intention. She had to somehow force herself to play the femme fatale with this overbearing boor. "My point was that I'm not very good at outdoor activities."

"Indoor games being your specialty, in other words."

"Something like that," she crooned, closing her eyes and tilting her head back provocatively to breathe in the night air. It was all she could do to keep from cringing at her own reckless performance. This was not exactly her most proficient talent, and she had had very little opportunity to practice this particular skill.

There was only a momentary flash of fear in her mind when she thought of how she could avoid making payment on this deal. She didn't really have a clear-cut plan for that yet, but surely she could think of something.

"So you don't want to get hurt." Michael nodded and bit his bottom lip as if he were deliberating something. "Okay, I'll tell you what. I promise I won't let you fall off a cliff."

"That's not exactly what I had in mind," she said through clenched teeth, trying to remain patient with this backwoods idiot who appeared patently ignorant about her more subtle meanings.

"Oh, sorry." He appeared contrite. "I thought you—"

"I don't want to have to do those things—any of them. I don't want to have to crawl and leap and—and rappel, and whatever else you seem intent on making us do. I don't want to do it. Do you understand what I'm saying?" She was trying desperately to keep the hysteria out of her voice.

"You're afraid," he spoke softly, still angry over her motives for this performance yet wanting, at the same time, to take her in his arms and shield her from all those things that frightened her so.

God, was he thick! "Yes. Yes, I'm afraid. All I want... from you... is for you to go easy on me. Don't make me do all those things. Please!" Damn! She hadn't intended to beg. This was turning out all wrong. She had to regain her control over the situation.

"And if I go easy on you?" His hand had moved back to her robe, this time his fingers sliding down the vee opening between her breasts.

"I..." Why did he have to touch her? Why couldn't he just listen? She was finding it extremely difficult to formulate coherent thoughts and sentences when he insisted on overpowering her this way. "I thought... that maybe I... I could relieve some of your... loneliness."

"You'll have sex with me." His voice was flat and level and unemotional. She grimaced over his phrasing of her proposal. Did he have to put it so crudely? He made it sound like she did this sort of thing for a living. But at least she had him thinking along the right line now.

She nodded demurely in answer to his question, then lowered her eyes.

Michael felt the pounding of his heart beneath his rib cage, and it took every ounce of control in his body to contain the combined forces of lust and anger toward this woman. Well, he would show her that he was one man she was not going to manipulate. This was his dominion and she was going to learn here and now that, for at least the next seven days, he was lord and master of her fate.

"I just want to make sure I've got this straight, okay?" The husky quality of his voice vibrated along her nerve endings.

Okay, okay. How bright could this guy be if he still wasn't sure what she was talking about?

His left hand lifted to grasp the other lapel on her robe, both hands sliding up and down the fabric. His voice dropped to a low whisper. "If I help you through the course and go easy on you, you will, in return, become mine... to do with whatever I want." The last phrase was a low, breathless rush of words. .

She shivered. Why all of a sudden did she feel she had gotten into water that was rising over her head? Had she, in truth, just made a bargain with the devil himself? "That's right," she braved, hating herself for having to resort to such a maneuver.

"When I want it and how I want it," Michael added, a note of warning somewhere adrift in the statement.

Evelyn's blue eyes widened in fear for only a second, before her self-assurance reclaimed her expression. *Dream on, Michael Baylor.* "Yes," she whispered with just the right amount of affected modesty.

"I didn't hear you."

"Yes," she repeated impatiently.

"Good." Before she was aware of what was happening, he was unzipping her robe and his right hand snaked inside the opening, closing around the soft mound of her breast. His other hand reached up behind her head, his fingers wrapping tightly in the strands of long, black hair.

Her face registered the shock of seeing the unerring descent of his mouth toward hers. She twisted sideways, her hand reaching up to grasp the arm that had made its way inside her robe. "What are you doing?" she gasped.

His mouth was only inches from hers when he spoke. "There's only one stipulation to the bargain, Evelyn." She stiffened at the ominous tone in his voice.

"Stipulation?" she asked, a growing wariness forming tight knots in her stomach and working its way upward to her throat. What did he mean by that? What else could he possibly want? And who was he to make stipulations to her anyway?

His voice was low and gravelly in her ear. "I expect payment in advance. Now."

Chapter Three

"Now?" her mouth screamed, though no discernible sound was emitted from her throat. Everything had suddenly gone haywire. This wasn't the way the scenario was supposed to play. Michael had switched the tactical maneuvers, new perimeters and lines of demarcation were drawn, and Evelyn was suddenly left with no ammunition.

"Michael!" Her voice finally penetrated the shocked blockage in her throat. "Please," she entreated with the proper tone of indignity. She had never intended to follow through on her bet. She hadn't realized that he would presume so much. How was it that other women were able to get away with tricks like this when she couldn't? What on earth was she going to do now?

She knew she had to string him along, making sure that he thought that she wasn't rebuffing his attempts all together, just wanting to slow things down a bit. "My," she sighed, "you're going a little too fast for me." She tried to gently shove him away, but she quickly realized she might as well have been trying to move Mt. Rushmore.

"Where's all that confidence you project so boldly now, Evelyn?" Both hands had moved to her bare waist, clenching her sides in the grip of his iron fingers. He sounded amused and yet his voice carried a tinge of anger. "We made a deal, remember? A business proposition. A contract, if you will. We both know the terms of the contract and the price to be paid, so there's really no sense in haggling over the date of delivery."

Her senses were spinning. The man was talking more like an attorney than a wilderness instructor. And his hands...the way they kept kneading the flesh of her sides. The large fingers probed into the curve of her hips, pulling her into his pelvis, a bold assertion that, at least to him, this was no game.

"I think you must have misunderstood what I was offering," she tried, sneaking a surreptitious look at him to see how her statement washed. It didn't.

His narrowed, steel-bladed eyes and tightly held jaw were the physical manifestations of the thin line she was walking with this man's temper. What would he be like if she pushed him too far? Would he be the type to force his will upon her? She had to think! Damn it, why wouldn't her brain function properly? If he would just remove his hands, those fingers that were making small circles on her flesh. As she waited with bated breath for his next reaction, she saw the look in his eye change from one of almost angry lust to one of cool, calculating decisiveness.

Immediately his hands were withdrawn from her robe, the fingers slowly and with precise deliberation pulling up the zipper to a stop just between her breasts. One finger brushed a soft tantalizing pattern against the skin at that spot, while his eyes never ceased their unnerving stare into her own.

"We'll change the conditions of the contract a little,

Evelyn." The cool, decisive tone left no room for re-
buttal. "When you decide that you want to play by my
rules—the only rules I play—then I'll uphold my end of
the agreement."

Evelyn stared wide-eyed, a feeling of hopeless defeat
washing over her. His rules? She had never played by
any but her own. It wasn't in her nature to be a fol-
lower. She had always been known, since she was a
young child, as a born leader. And she had never met
any one before that she couldn't lead. Until now.

"The problem is that you're not really sure if you
want this," he was saying, with total self-assurance.
"But by tomorrow night or the next night..." He
paused for effect, watching the fearful shudder that rip-
pled through her body. "By then, you'll be ready to
play the game."

That was all it took. His smug assertion that she
couldn't handle the physical stress of the program and
would willingly fall into his arms to avoid it was the
electrical jolt that prodded her ego back into gear. Dis-
regarding the fact that she was the one who said she
couldn't take the physical hardships and that she was
the one who made the bargain in the first place, Evelyn
glared at Michael as if he had just suggested something
that was completely absurd and disgusting.

"Never!" she cried, pushing herself away from him
and running down the steps and back across the cold
ground to her cabin. Before entering the cabin, she
chanced one more glance in his direction. He was leaning against the railing, his body seemingly casual and
aloof. But he was watching her with those deep, metal-
lic eyes. That much she knew for sure.

Didn't Dorothy say this was the place to work off

one's frustrations? Funny, it seemed to Evelyn that they were just beginning.

Michael tried to slow his rapid heartbeat as he watched Evelyn run down the path. *Damn that woman!* She was turning him upside down and he wasn't going to stand for it. There was no way he was going to let her use him to get what she wanted. If she learned nothing else here, she was going to learn that life was a balance of give and take and that in nature there was no room for power plays. But how was he going to teach her this and what on earth was he going to do about his constant need to touch her?

An excited and nervous group gathered around the front steps of the lodge before daybreak. They were all there. All, that is, except Evelyn.

Each person was handed a glass of orange juice by a small, round woman with dark, graying hair pulled tightly into a bun on the back of her head. As soon as the tray of juice was emptied, she retreated into the lodge and quickly returned with another tray brimming with bagels and cream cheese.

Butterflies were rampant in the participants' stomachs this morning, making it difficult to think about food. But Michael's advice that they would need the energy later forced them all to down the juice and rolls.

At twenty minutes past four, Evelyn finally appeared. Her raven hair had been tied at the back of her head, one long braid hanging down between her shoulder blades. She was dressed in khaki-colored bermuda shorts with a suede, royal-blue belt and her shirt was a soft blue chambray with long sleeves that she knew she could roll up later when the day became too warm. On her feet were knee-length argyle socks and brown suede hiking shoes that she had just purchased through Bergdorf's new safari collection.

Her makeup, as always, was pure perfection. Her light brown eyeshadow filled the lower lid, sweeping up to join the darker cinnamon that lined the crease. Her lipstick was chosen with the outing in mind. Not wanting to look like she was prepared for a day in the city, she chose a shade of lip coloring in the brown family, with just a hint of copper.

She had deliberated long and hard on her attire for the day, picking up and discarding several possible choices until she found the one suitable outfit. But, as she now approached the stupefied group, she wondered if she could have possibly made an error in judgment.

They were all looking at her, gawking, staring, disbelieving. Only when she noticed their mode of dress, did she realize the mistake she had made. The rest of the members of the group were dressed in faded jeans, western or flannel shirts, heavy-duty socks and boots or calf-high hiking shoes.

"You're late." Michael glared at her, then began to shake his head in disbelief. "What in the hell do you have on?"

Her face paled and she remained silent. She had never felt so out of place in her life. Always before, she had been praised for her flair for dressing. Both the men and the women she socialized with all had a rare sense of style. But suddenly it was as if this particular ability was a drawback and her mind was frantically trying to search for an explanation. How could that be so?

"Go back to your cabin and put on some long jeans," Michael ordered.

And look like the rest of you misfits? No way. "I'll stay the way I am, thank you." It wasn't so much that she thought she was right. It was that she would, in no way, back down like some whimpering coward from that overbearing despot.

The two adversaries glared at each other for several long seconds, each weighing the power of the other. It was hard to even look at Michael this morning after what had taken place between them last night. She felt her skin growing warm with embarrassment and anger as she thought of his hands so bold and hot, invading inside her robe. And one look at his shining cobalt eyes told her he was remembering the same thing. She turned her head quickly to avoid the brunt of his thoughts, whatever they might be. But despite the awkwardness of their situation, she was not going to let him boss her around. She had too much pride for that.

In the end, and to her complete surprise, it was Michael who backed down. He turned back to the rest of the group and, without another word, began loading his pack onto his back. The other members of the brigade kept their vague conjectures to themselves and loaded their packs as their leader had done.

Evelyn noticed the empty glasses on the tray on the front step. "Do I not get some breakfast?"

"You were late, Scott." Michael helped Frank lift his pack onto his shoulders. "Here, everything is done on schedule. If you miss out on something, that's the breaks."

Yeah? Well, I'd like to break your neck. How was she supposed to make it through the day without at least a cup of coffee? She could feel the rumblings already beginning in her stomach. But there was no way she would give him the satisfaction of knowing how hungry she was. So, swallowing a ravenous growl, she began putting on her gear.

Struggling with her pack, she managed, with no small amount of difficulty, to heave it onto her shoulders, already aghast at how heavy it felt on her back. Pulling the belt around to the front, she tried to loop the end through the unusual buckle fastening.

After working unsuccessfully for several minutes to fasten it, a pair of strong, tanned hands reached for the ends and with ease looped the end of the belt through the buckle and cinched it tightly against her waist.

While those large hands were touching her, she did not move. She did not even breathe. Unable to look at his face, she watched his hands as they worked, the brown weathered skin, the large fingers that seemed to have already staked a claim on her body. When she finally glanced up at him, she saw the gleam of laughter in his eyes. He knew full well the uncomfortable effect he was having on her, and he was enjoying every sadistic minute of it.

"Surrender, Evelyn. Accept the fact that you will never win this game."

She glowered at him. Never would she surrender! Just because he was bigger than she was, she would not cower under his imperious attitude. She could hold her own with any man. And that's all Michael Baylor was— just a man. The fact that he was more man than she had ever known before was an unwanted thought that crouched in the forefront of her mind and would not allow itself to be dislodged.

Michael watched her closely for a moment then stepped away, and Evelyn berated herself for the psychological fear that some vital support, some lifeline to her being, had just been severed.

The rest of the team seemed oblivious to what had just taken place as they busied themselves with adjusting packs and with excited chatter. Even Michael, as he moved through the group, appeared to have conveniently pushed her out of his mind.

"Is everybody ready?" He smiled wickedly. Answered by groans and negative replies, he laughed. "Well, at least you're all honest." He flicked a cursory glance at Evelyn, as if he were excluding her from this observation.

Heading out of the base camp with his seven charges in tow, he talked again about what they would be doing today and the skills he would be teaching.

"We'll be heading northeast for the first half-mile or so. Keep an eye on your compasses so that you know where we are going at all times."

"G.I. Joe will probably get lost and we'll have to lead him back to camp," Evelyn muttered to John who was walking just in front of her.

He turned and laughed with her.

"Evelyn always knows where she's going, don't you Evelyn?" Frank hollered tauntingly back at her from the front of the line.

"I hope you're the first to fall over a cliff, Frank," she said.

Heading down a narrow footpath through the pines, Evelyn glanced back to get her last glimpse at the lodge. It wasn't too late to turn back. Was it? As she blindly followed the three men in front of her, the question was unceremoniously left behind in the dirt.

After only fifteen minutes, she realized the importance of Michael's advice about the packs. Her bag was cutting into her shoulders and forcing her head down so that all she could see was the ground. Would it, she wondered, permanently cause a stoop? But it was just as well she had to look down. For every time she caught a glimpse of Michael's snug-fitting jeans beneath his pack, she felt her strength wearing away even faster.

For an hour, they walked at an even pace on relatively flat ground. It was a peaceful morning, the sun making a slow ascent above the tall spruce trees, and the forest was softened by the early morning mist. The grass was still damp and silvery with dew, and with each footstep, the soft fragrance of wild flowers and the spicy yet sweet scent of pine needles was stirred into the thin air.

Evelyn tried to enjoy the scenery and discover some redeeming factor in all of this torture. But it was difficult, if not impossible.

As they walked through high weeds, her knees were scratched and tickled constantly by the tall grasses and thorns from wild roses. Her blouse was now clinging to her body from perspiration, but the weight of the pack made it seem impossible to lift her arms to roll up her cuffs. And, above all else, she was starving.

After what seemed to Evelyn like a full day's hike, but in actuality was only two hours, Michael stopped and let everyone sit and rest.

"I suggest you leave your packs on," he advised, as they found several boulders on which to sit.

"Aren't we going to camp here?" The boy scout leader from Kansas was heaving breathlessly.

Michael looked over the physical state of his charges and laughed. Everyone laughed with him, without the faintest clue as to why they did so. "Hardly" was his only reply.

Evelyn worked for two full minutes to pull a pack of cigarettes from her side pocket, then shook one out into her hand. As it touched her mouth, she heard a stern, "No."

"What?"

"No smoking."

"You've got to be kidding!" He had to be kidding! She had been doing well to make it for two hours without a cigarette.

"No," he answered. "I'm not kidding. At this altitude, you're going to need all the oxygen you can get. Smoking only cuts down on that oxygen."

"You mean, we're not to smoke...at all?" John Stimmer asked, his fingers already nervously twirling a long blade of grass.

"That's right. No cigarettes."

"Why didn't you tell us that yesterday?" asked Bill Adler.

"If I had told you then, you would have fretted and stewed about it all night. This way, it's easier. You have no other choice." He grinned as if it amused him to torture his victims this way.

Evelyn played with the unlit cigarette between her fingers. He couldn't do this to them. Could he? She had tried to quit smoking several years ago, but she turned into such a grouch that the people who worked for her in her office finally bought her a pack of cigarettes because they couldn't stand being around her anymore.

Her mind zeroed in on the memory of last night. She had seen Michael sitting on the porch smoking a cigarette when she walked up to him. How could he stop smoking so easily? Her mind began to whirl suspiciously. I'll bet he sneaks off in the trees when we're not looking and lights up a cigarette. That sneak... Well, she would just have to keep an eye on him. He wasn't going to get away with any double crosses as long as she was there to keep tabs on him.

Michael watched Evelyn fuming on her boulder, and he smiled inwardly. He could almost see the gears in her mind working overtime as she plotted and schemed against him. After the ten-minute break, he pulled some sheets of paper from his pocket, handing one to each person.

"Today is what I call Cold Turkey Day... in more ways than one," he laughed, as he watched John chewing ferociously on a blade of grass. "How many of you have ever been on a treasure hunt?"

Several of the members confirmed that they had, but it had been twenty or thirty years ago. Evelyn said nothing. She was staring with sullen bewilderment at the piece of paper in her hands. Whatever obscure message was on the sheet of paper was not only scribbled almost illegibly, but it was also written in an unfamiliar language.

"The treasure"—Michael grinned mischievously— "is hot food and a nice... soft... comfortable place to sleep." He could see now that he had everyone's attention, so he continued. "To find it, you might need canoes."

"Might?"

"Am I not speaking distinctly, Scott?"

Evelyn gritted her teeth, holding in her sarcastic comeback.

"Now," he continued, "watch my lips: You might need canoes. To find the campsite, you will use the clues and instructions I've issued to each of you. But here's the catch. There will be no—I repeat no—talking except to read aloud the message written on your piece of paper. Ready to begin?"

"How am I supposed to read this? I don't even know what language it's in." Evelyn glared at Michael, a vague uneasiness settling over her. Maybe she should have accepted his sexual attentions last night. Maybe she should have played her hand a little differently. Well, it was too late now. She would just have to plow through this silly little treasure hunt with the rest of the group.

"It's Portuguese, and I'm sure you'll manage it like you do everything else, Scott. With inimitable style. Now, Stimmer, why don't you read your message first and we'll go down the line." He had dismissed her and her question as inconsequential. He was even calling her Scott now. God, she disliked that man!

"Mine says that the water in the creek is between fifty and fifty-five degrees. What creek?" Everyone looked around for the cleverly concealed water.

"Ah, remember the rules?" Michael smiled. "No talking except to read your message."

Everyone groaned, except Michael who, of course, chuckled to himself. They went down the line, each of them reading their instructions.

"The compass bearing at the starting point is north, northwest."

"The creek flows on a southeasterly course."

"The treasure is located at nine thousand, three hundred and fifty-five feet in elevation."

"The treasure is exactly one and one-half miles from the starting point."

Evelyn glowered at Michael before sighing and struggling to read her message. *"O acampamento fica a cem pasos de uma velha mina de ouro."*

"Very good, Scott," Michael clapped.

Everyone began to giggle nervously over the game. Everyone, that is, except Evelyn. She continued to glare at Michael as if it were all his fault that she had to partake in this childish game. Why couldn't he have just accepted the bargain as she intended it? Why did he think he had to run the whole show?

Not knowing where to begin, the members of the brigade wandered aimlessly around the resting area for a few minutes. Finally, Charles Stipple signaled silently for everyone to follow him.

A major problem suddenly became evident to the members of the group. With each of them leaders in their own corporate environments, none of them particularly wanted to be followers now. Thus, it was a disgruntled group who begrudgingly followed Charles down the path he had chosen. But it soon became obvious that Charles didn't know where the hell he was going any more than the rest of them, so they eventually tended to drift in their own separate ways.

From the beginning of this silly little game, Evelyn had been conscious of Michael trailing behind them. She turned once to look at him and was infuriated by the unconcealed amusement written in every line of his face. She tried to forget he was there. She tried not to imagine his face in front of her, his hands on her waist, the bold pressure of his hips against hers. She tried not to think of his lips so near her own. *Keep your mind on this stupid task at hand, Evelyn. Don't think about those eyes, so gemlike, framed in thick, dark lashes, drilling into your back right now. Don't think at all. Just move.*

Two hours later, the group members were still milling around and lost. Tempers were short and everyone was completely exhausted and discouraged. Still smiling roguishly, Michael finally offered much needed help.

"Follow me." Everyone was too exhausted and hungry to argue and now each corporate chief was more than ready to become a mere Indian.

Plunging through the thickly wooded forest for almost a mile, Michael led them to a swollen, rapidly flowing creek. The sound of the silvery water playing over the rocks almost drowned out their cries of relief. Rushing to the bank, they each cupped their hands and began sucking in the cool, clear water. No one noticed that Dorothy did not join in the spree, but instead stood next to Michael with her arms folded across her chest, wearing an expression of supreme superiority.

"Wait a minute," Michael warned. "Don't drink so much of that."

"I thought there was no cleaner water in the world," Frank countered.

"That's a common misconception. There are campsites farther upstream and there are also herds of sheep that graze along here." As if struck by a lightning bolt, everyone jumped back from the creek, horrified expressions beginning to cover their faces.

Michael laughed. "Don't worry about it, for goodness' sakes. Just use common sense. Most people think that because it's a mountain stream, it's pure water. Well, as the song goes, it ain't necessarily so. Now, when we get higher up, the water will be cleaner and we'll have facilities to boil it. But, for now, use your canteens. That's why you have them."

"Where are the canoes?" Evelyn's hands were on her hips, disgust etched into every line of her tightly held expression.

"Canoes?" Michael feigned ignorance.

"I thought we were supposed to find canoes." All of the short-tempered hikers were beginning to get hostile.

"I said you might. Look at this creek." Michael walked to the edge and pointed. "Look at the rocks on the bottom. Do you see how shallow it is? Do you really think you could use canoes in that?" Michael tapped his forehead with an index finger, indicating that they had better start using that space between their ears for something other than forming complaints.

"Then, what? Why?"

Michael shrugged his shoulders and said nothing, heading instead across the creek, everyone fording the stream in a foul mood behind him.

"I'll get my shoes wet!" Evelyn cried, standing on the opposite bank from the others.

"Boo! Hoo!" Frank yelled sarcastically.

Michael walked back to the bank, his eyebrow arching in impatience. "What's the problem, Scott?"

"I'll ruin my shoes."

"Scott, if this is a joke, everyone's tired and—"

"I'll ruin my shoes!"

"Well, what in the hell did you bring Gucci shoes for anyway?"

"They're not Guccis."

"Damn!" Michael muttered turning to walk back to

the head of the line. "I'm not going to argue with you anymore, Evelyn. I don't care how you do it, just get your butt across the creek."

Oh, that... ! How dare he? Oh, how she despised him! This was torture. She shouldn't have to do this sort of thing. She didn't even want to be here. Why was she being punished so? Her chest heaved in anger and inside she ranted and raved, silently heaping every curse she could think of upon Michael's head.

When she finally realized that he was not going to help her, she sat down on the bank and began furiously removing her shoes and socks. Holding them in her arms, she sank one leg two feet into the icy creek, chill bumps immediately covering her entire body. Putting the other foot in next, she slowly gained her balance and gingerly began making her way along the slippery rocks to the other side.

As she made it to the opposite edge, John Stimmer's hand reached out to help her up onto the bank. But instead of warming her soul, his sympathetic gesture chilled her to the bone. She didn't want his sympathy, damn it. She didn't want anything to do with any of them. They were all against her. She could tell that now. They were the enemy and she'd be damned if she'd accept their aid. She would show them that she didn't need their help.

She jerked her hand away from John's and glared at Michael who was standing a few feet away. Though his mouth was set in a tight line, the slightly narrowed flashing eyes were filled with an implied invitation, one that clearly stated, "Any time you're ready to accept the bargain on my terms, Evelyn, just let me know."

She really detested him.

After hiking along a steep incline for another hour, then wading waist deep through a log-jammed beaver pond, the cold, wet, and hungry brigade finally stumbled onto their treasure—that night's campground. In disagreeable silence, the group members each unrolled their bedding, started a fire and, with minimum conversation, divided up chores of cooking, cleaning, and wood gathering. Once they were all agreed as to who was going to do what and had begun heating a reconstituted vegetable protein packet labeled "ham" over the campfire, Michael sat down on a tree stump before them.

"I think we should talk about what this morning was all about," he suggested, and his gentle tone was an obvious attempt at a peace offering.

"We weren't supposed to find our campsite, were we?" Bill Adler's voice was bitter with accusation, then the others chimed in.

"What was the point?"

"That was a cruel trick."

"The idea"—Michael interrupted this tirade by standing and adding some more kindling to the fire—"was for you to start off with a collective task, something you could all work together on."

"How could we work together? We couldn't even talk."

"Just because you can't talk does not mean you can't communicate." Michael's gaze locked with Evelyn's as if he were now speaking to her alone. "Sometimes the words we use mask what we're really trying to say. This is something I want you to learn at the outset. Believe me, tomorrow will be better."

"Well, I for one have nothing to say to any of you.

Period," Evelyn huffed as she stalked off with her aluminum plate full of mysterious-looking food and plopped down in a private shaded spot under a pine tree.

The rest of the day was spent in camp learning how to tie knots in their ropes, how to restuff their packs so that the weight was distributed more evenly, and how to cope with the cold-turkey withdrawal from nicotine.

By late afternoon, humor had still not returned to the group of misfits. Evelyn continued to isolate herself from the rest and attempted in disgruntled fashion to learn how to master timber hitches and bowlines.

"Just remember"—Michael knelt down beside her and took the rope from her hands, his disturbingly powerful presence stretching her already taut nerves to the breaking point—"the rabbit comes out of the hole, goes around the tree, and goes back in the hole."

She grabbed the rope from him in disgust. What kind of a moron did he think she was? she scowled and cursed his entire being as she repeatedly tried to make the rabbit go out, around, and in the hole.

By nightfall, after a hot meal of "Good and Plenty Chicken," complete and utter weariness had settled over the group. Walter Green, the paunchy scout leader, was the first to find good use for his sleeping bag, but the others followed close behind him.

As Evelyn lay in her lumpy bedroll, with its too-tight liner, and stared up at the vast expanse of sky, the sleeping sounds of the other members in the group did not encourage her to join their ranks. She was tired. No, she was exhausted. But the aches that racked every square inch of her body made it impossible to find a comfortable position in which to lie. And, too, her convoluted thoughts about their intrepid, lionhearted leader kept her mind from finding the peace that only sleep could bring.

She had to find a way out of this living nightmare, and at every spinning revolution of her thoughts, she knew the only way out was through Michael. Yet, at the same time, she didn't want to let him win. It had become a much larger war than the one that had begun last night. Now, it was going to be a fight to the finish between two perversely determined people, neither of whom would ever willingly accept defeat.

A dark silhouette knelt down beside her. He smiled at her, gently this time. Her facial muscles did not move. She wanted to find something cruel to say to him. Some way to hurt him the way she had been hurt. But something devastating happened to her whenever he looked at her. No man had ever affected her in that way. Instead of wanting to hurt him, she suddenly thought of taking her arm from under her sleeping bag and reaching out to stroke his neck. She remembered from the evening in New York what it felt like to run her fingers through his thick brown hair and she could still taste the warmth of his mouth on hers. What was in his unflinching, dark-lashed eyes? What were they saying to her?

"How do you feel, Evelyn?"

She stared at him, trying to decide if he disliked her as much as she disliked him. "Rotten." The bewitching spell was at last broken and her anger was allowed free reign. "That was a stupid game you played today."

"Oh, don't be a poor sport, love."

"Do not call me that," she hissed through tight lips. "I am not your love."

He shrugged as if her argument was insignificant. "Not yet, anyway."

"Never, Michael. Never. Ever." Forgetting for a moment the racking pain in every muscle fiber of her body, she gloated, "I made it just fine without your help today."

Michael leaned closer to her, letting his fire-lit eyes rake over her body with infinite leisure, devouring the curves he imagined there to be under the covers, before stopping on her face. His hand reached up to finger one long strand in the mass of black hair that had loosened from the braid and tumbled around her head. The feel of its silky texture in his hands caused the blood to bound through his veins. She was so beautiful to look at and he wanted to show her what she had done to him today. He wanted her to know how difficult it was to be around her and not take her in his arms. And yet, he couldn't give her any advantage. Not until he had taught her that sometimes we find that what we've been fighting for all along is not at all what we really want or need.

Evelyn's breath caught in her throat as she watched his eyes roaming across her face and body, and that wild need began to beat inside of her again.

When he spoke, his voice was like a rush of wind through the pine trees. "You know, Evelyn, today you may have won the battle, but have no doubt about this — I will win the war."

As she stared up at that determined countenance, Evelyn experienced a rare moment of truth with herself and knew deep inside that Michael Baylor was probably right.

Chapter Four

The low, masculine sound that penetrated the fog of her sleep-laden mind was both pleasant and annoying. The voice itself sent warm vibrations coursing through her body, but it was the cold gravity of the words themselves that tended to grate on her nerves.

Evelyn opened her eyes slowly to the new day—the brand-spanking new day, she reflected grimly, seeing only a vague flush of light over the tops of the pine trees. It couldn't be much later than five o'clock in the morning, and the voice that was filling her body cavity with such delicious sensations was Michael's. What was he saying? Oh wonderful, he was reading more rules! How could there be any more rules than there already were?

No smoking. No alcohol. Never hike alone. All decisions will be group decisions. . . .

"Ouch!" Evelyn jumped to a sitting position, glaring at the man who had just given her bottom a tremendous wallop with the palm of his hand.

"Rise and shine, princess." Michael laughed at her indignant expression as he walked over to stir the freeze-dried eggs simmering in an aluminum pan over the fire.

The rest of the team members were already up and bustling about so Evelyn, swallowing her bruised pride and rubbing her tender bottom, slowly forced her still tired body from the bedroll. Ignoring the cheerful greetings from Dorothy the linebacker and Walter the Boy Scout, Evelyn walked stiffly on aching legs into the trees to nature's latrine.

Yesterday, when she had first realized that there were no restrooms or even outhouses along the route, she had been ready to throw up her arms in defeat and head straight back to civilization. She didn't. But all the same, she questioned her sanity in remaining a part of this masochistic cluster, the nucleus of which was a man whose sole purpose in life seemed to be to devise intricate means of torture for his captive charges. Was it some sort of perverse desire to undergo such torture that kept her going on this ridiculous expedition? Or was it that she secretly and unconsciously delighted in waging this war with Michael? Whatever it was, it kept her feet moving steadily onward.

While the enemy—as she now silently referred to the rest of the group—prepared a hearty breakfast, Evelyn sat cross-legged on her sleeping bag, pulled out her travel mirror and began sorting through her makeup with all the deliberation of an artist in front of her colorful palette. She had just decided which eyeshadow to use when a huge, brown leather boot swept furiously across her bedroll, scattering the assorted tubes and pencils and creams about the campsite.

"What—what on earth are you doing?" Evelyn's voice was a shrill reflection of her shock.

"No more, Evelyn." Michael's stance was tense and unflinching, as if something highly explosive inside of him was about to blow.

"Who do you think you are, telling me what to do?" She knew, by the granite-hard glaze in his eyes, that she was probably pushing his temper too far, but she couldn't stop. She continued to rant and yell, standing and kicking dirt onto his boots in a feeble and childish attempt to get back at him.

In swift, precise movements, he grasped her upper arm in an iron grip, reached down to pick up the mirror that had been spared from his boot, then dragged her with him toward a stand of trees. When they were hidden from the curious eyes of the rest of the group, he stopped and turned her toward him.

"Look in there. Look!" He forced the mirror up in front of her face. "What do you see? Go on, look."

She tried to shrug her arm free from his grasp, but it was hopeless. His hand was like a steel vise squeezing the strength from her muscles and flesh. She looked into the mirror reluctantly, as if she were afraid of what she might see. But reflected in the glass was nothing more frightening than the image of Evelyn Scott.

She examined herself closely. Strands of black hair had loosened from the single braid and were dangling about her neck. Her skin was a bit sallow from the cold night air, but it looked younger and smoother than her thirty-one years. There were no wrinkles, no hollows or shadows; it was soft and clear. Her light blue eyes looked tired from the short night, but that was to be expected, and her lips were pale peach, a not so inappropriate color for this natural setting.

She glanced awkwardly back at Michael. Without her

awareness, he had loosened his hold on her arm and was lightly stroking the flesh above her elbow. "Do you see what I see?" he whispered in a deep, male caress.

Her gaze flickered to his eyes, wondering, anxious, yet curious for his assessment of her.

"You're beautiful, Evelyn. You don't need to hide behind those masks you paint on every morning." He lightly stroked her cheek with the back of his knuckles. "Don't pretend to be something you're not. Be what you are."

She looked back into the mirror at her reflection. She had to admit that he was right. She did look fine the way she was. She had always assumed that she needed all that makeup, that it enhanced her beauty, hid her flaws. But perhaps she had been hiding what she really was from everyone, even from herself. Maybe, just maybe, Michael was right.

"How do you know what I am?" She tried, with little success, to retain some of her indignation.

"I know you a lot better than you may think, Evelyn. Maybe a lot better than you know yourself." He combed his fingers through one of the black wisps of hair that had fallen across her face, brushing it back from her forehead.

Yes, he knew her. Everytime he caught a glimpse of her determined stride, or heard the impatient lack of tolerance in her voice, or watched her trying to massage away the tension in her temples, he was seeing himself the way he had been a few years ago. He too had been a hard-charger, had ridden the fast track to success. But no more. He had seen the devastating results of that side of life. He was on the other side now.

And he would never go back. Yes, he knew Evelyn Scott. Much better than she knew herself.

Evelyn was aware of a weakness flooding through her limbs as Michael continued to brush his fingers through her hair. To give in to the feeling, that riveting masculine dominance, to let happen whatever was natural...

No! She couldn't! Michael was still the archenemy. She knew what he was trying to pull. He wanted her; that much was obvious. And he seemed determined to have her. No doubt he had some bet with Josh and the other instructors over how long it would take for him to win her over. And she had played right into his hands by making that stupid bargain. All she wanted to do was go back to New York, back to the elements she understood. But Michael was trying to turn her into something she couldn't possibly be.

"It's not going to work," she ventured with a caustic sting.

"What isn't?" He seemed genuinely perplexed.

"This little campaign of yours. Your strategy is to win the war, as you so honestly admitted last night. And I'm the war, am I not, Michael?"

His gaze blazed a slow, searing trail down her body, then ascended by inches until it came to rest on her mouth. She knew exactly what was going to happen, even before his mouth descended with single-minded determination toward her tightly clamped lips.

Breathing soft words onto her flesh, he affirmed, "Yes, Evelyn, you are most definitely the war."

His mouth brushed across the surface of her lips, leisurely, softening and shaping them to fit his own. With ease, born of his natural ability and practiced skill, he tasted and caressed the surface of her lips until, without a struggle, they opened to him.

A series of shock waves reverberated through her body as his tongue plunged into the interior of her mouth and began exploring its depths as thoroughly and lovingly as if he were seeking some priceless treasure within her being.

She had not meant to wrap her arms around his neck that way, nor had she purposely meant to press the lower half of her body against his. It had just happened. Something vibrantly warm within her was more powerful than all her good intentions. She had forged into the battleground and was overcome by the explosive sensations around her. But, at the same time, something in the more rational sectors of her brain continued to scream for retreat.

Abruptly, she pulled away, startling both Michael and this new, unfamiliar and reckless self who lived within her body. "No, Michael!"

She cringed inside to think what she had done. She had divulged the secrets of her weakness to the enemy, giving him a decided margin of advantage over her. She was a traitor to her soul. But she would remedy that. She must. Her face and body again hardened with renewed determination.

"I'm not the weak little helpless creature you all think I am. And believe me, the war is not over yet. In fact, it hasn't even begun." With one last glower in his direction, she retreated from the battlefront. Back in the campsite with the others she would be safe. Safety in numbers would be her fortification.

If she had seen the smile that lifted Michael's mouth as he watched her retreat, she might not have felt so secure. His indistinct remark was carried off by the wind through the pines, never reaching her ears.

"That's right, Evelyn Scott. You are no helpless creature. And before this course is over, you will have even convinced yourself of that."

After the brigade members loaded their gear, they marched out of camp. This day was a repeat of the day before—only worse. More strenuous. More grueling. More painful. But again that night, Evelyn found herself unable to fall asleep peacefully like the others. Her mind was filled with bewildering thoughts of one man, with how she could be attracted to someone she disliked so much. He was everything she had always tried to avoid. Physical work is obsolete, her overbearing aunt had drilled into her head again and again. Life is too short to kill yourself with ambition, Michael would say.

Why had she come here? Why had she allowed herself to be manipulated in this way? Questions without answers plagued her second night in the wilderness, but out of sheer physical exhaustion, she finally was able to sleep.

By the third morning, the group had established certain routines for cooking and cleaning, and the days began to fall into an orderly, if still disagreeable, pattern.

On the third day, after the campsite was cleaned, the brigade again headed out. Today, somewhere out there, awaited that vague, mysterious terror known as the "ropes course."

But before they reached this gloomy region of hell, they had to wade through an icy creek, then jog—packs and all—three quarters of a mile through the dense, ever-climbing forest. To Evelyn's increasing irritation, Michael, for some reason, felt it part of his job to point out where deer bedded down for the night, label the hundreds of varieties of wild flowers they passed, and explain nature's ecological system for replenishing a forest after a fire.

"These are lodge-pole pine," he would explain, picking up a hard, brown seed. "They are so tough to crack that it takes the intense heat from a forest fire to do it. When an area has been decimated by fire, these lodge-pole are the first to grow and reforest the mountains."

After each one of these enlightening forestry lessons, Evelyn would roll her eyes. She had to admit, they were interesting facts to know if one's only goal was to trip through life picking wild flowers like some wood nymph. She, Evelyn Scott, did not have that kind of time.

Michael was trying to force her to coast. How could she make him understand that if she slowed down, she would be forced to think about what was going to happen in two years or three years. She would have to face the fact that she might never have a man to love her, a family to care for. She was used to filling her mind with so many business activities that she would not have to think about the future. But seven days without her work to distract her! How could she make it without those nagging doubts and worries entering her mind?

In a perverted twist of justice, she was relieved of too much introspection by the pain of the present. The heavy load, plus the continual upswing in altitude sapped her energy and her ever-lessening supply of oxygen. Again, the position of the pack on her back pushed her head down where she could only see her own feet plodding along, and her clothes were soaked from continual wades through frigid streams.

Glancing at her hands, she noticed ruefully that four of her beautifully tapered nails had broken to the quick. The others were split badly and the polish was chipping loose. Her only sense of victory was in knowing that Michael had been wrong as to the time when the nails would break. They had lasted a day and a half longer than he had predicted.

Above all else, the one thing that constantly kept her teetering on the brink of defeat was the vision of Michael's back in front of her. When she was able to lift her head enough to see in front of her, she would notice how his broad shoulders held the pack with the ease and comfort of one who had done this sort of thing all his life. And she hated him for it. She hated him for his lack of discomfort, for his self-assured ability, for his courage, and most of all for his compelling masculinity. The enemy. She had to remember that. He was the enemy!

When she was at the point where she thought she could not go another step, Michael led them into a large clearing, rimmed by spruce and aspen trees. But an empty clearing it was not. Before the dumbstruck group was a terrifying collection of equipment, myriad instruments of torture far surpassing anything Evelyn could have imagined.

She glanced at each of the other members of the group. All but two held expressions as terrified as her own. Michael folded his arms across his chest and smiled magnanimously, as if he were selflessly bestowing a yardful of toys for gleeful children. Dorothy imitated his stance and wore a smug expression of self-confidence that Evelyn would have liked to physically wipe off the woman's face.

Filling the gap of silent fear with his philosophical brand of calm assurance, Michael spoke. "The idea here is to give you a chance to see where your body is in space. These exercises are modeled after the Special Forces exercises used by the U.S. Army."

"You mean like military exercises? As in boot camp?" Evelyn's eyes were like those of a frightened doe.

"Yes. It's designed to demand the maximum from each participant." His eyes shifted to each member of the group before landing on Evelyn. They narrowed slightly as they examined her, as he tried to gauge what her physical limitations would be.

"What if we can't do it?" one of the men asked. Michael's attention swerved back to the others.

"Nothing on this course is beyond your capabilities. All of you can do it, if you tell yourself so."

Inside Evelyn's mind, the brain waves refused to agree. Her quivering inner voice began its repetitive chant. *I can't make it! I can't make it! I can't make it!*

The course consisted of fourteen separate tasks. While some were, in reality, relatively harmless, the entire course turned into a nightmarish binge in terror for Evelyn.

It was as if the day would last forever, as if this were her hell, this dimension of torture in which she must exist for all time. Never had she known so much pain or fatigue or hardship. And never would she forgive Michael for forcing her to undergo this experience in horror.

She would glare at him throughout the day, while he, in return, would smile with sadistic amusement, cocking his eyebrow to remind her that it had been her decision to back out of the bargain, and not his.

Once, he even had the audacity to whisper in her ear, asking her if she had changed her mind about their "little agreement." It was as if he were goading her on, baiting her with the full knowledge that she would defy him to the very end.

The exercises seemed to progress from the least taxing to the most. And, with each one, Evelyn felt the growing agony of defeat in her muscles and in her will.

But it was an incident entirely unrelated to the physical stress that seemed to stretch her endurance almost beyond the breaking point.

She was slipping on her harness for an exercise in which each of the participants would be tied together for the assault of a forty-foot-high slab of rock. As she tried to tie the harness around her waist, the nylon string caught on a button of her unbleached muslin shirt. While the other team members were busy with their own adjustments and procedures, Evelyn struggled in vain to loosen the tangled string and thread.

Michael noticed her struggles and began walking toward her. *Oh, damn,* she cried inwardly. She didn't want him to help her. She didn't want him touching her!

His hands reached out and brushed her frantic fingers aside.

"What seems to be the problem here, Scott?" His words were all business, but his voice was rich with low tones, husky and warmly inviting.

"It's this...this string...I..."

His hands were already working at the thread, unwinding and detangling, but his fingers seemed to spread further over the rise of her breasts than necessary for the task. The electric touch of his hands on her body sent flames of fire curling and licking through her veins. She felt the tips of her breasts stiffen, and she suffered the humiliation of watching Michael raise his head and stare knowingly into her eyes.

She tried to swallow, but a lump in her throat blocked the passage. His fingers were taking much too long to correct a simple little tangle. And did he have to put his face so close to the offending little button?

"Ah, here it is. The thread's caught," he stated the obvious, smiling devilishly as he did so. Assuming, hoping that he would quickly remedy the situation and then go away, Evelyn was dismayed and shocked when his mouth zeroed in on the button. Wrapping his arms around her waist, he caught the thread in his teeth and yanked. The action removed his head from her chest, but at the same time forced her pelvis tightly against his.

"Michael!" she hissed, trying to keep her voice from carrying to the other group members. She pushed against his shoulders, but he had not loosened his hold on her waist. She could feel an unwanted heat building around her thighs where they touched his. It was like being trapped inside a mountain, all around this huge presence holding you in, hugging you and suffocating you at the same time. "Let me go!" she whispered venomously.

He ignored her demands, his attention focused instead on the hollow between her breasts, on the feel of her abdomen against his.

"Damn it, Michael, let me go!"

He raised his eyes to her face and placed a roughly textured finger against her lips. "Shhh, Evelyn. Don't wear yourself out. You're going to need your strength for the rest of the course... that is, unless you've decided that defeat under me might not be so bad after all."

Defeat under Michael would be worse than bad. It would be devastating. Once she surrendered herself to a man like that, it might be irrevocable. As they stared at each other for one long, soul-penetrating moment before their bodies separated, it was as if they were both realizing this same irrefutable fact.

With ever-weakening resolve, Evelyn climbed the slab of rock with the others, took her turn in the "commando crawl," where she was required to inch along, in a prone position, a forty-foot rope strung ten feet off the ground. She was sent screaming down the tramway, a wire fastened fifty feet above ground with only a ten-inch wooden bar on which to hold. She completed them all, all the terrifying exercises that were supposed to give her more confidence in her ability to manage employees but, in effect, only made her more aware of her own limitations.

The final break in the communication between her brain and her body came at the "flea's leap," and, at that point, she knew she had lost the war.

Looking at it from below, it hadn't seemed like such an awesome task. It was merely a short hop from one rock ledge to another that was three feet away and two feet lower. But standing up there now looking down the deep crevice between the ledges, Evelyn knew it was more than simply an exercise. For her, it was suicide, pure and simple.

She tried to make the jump once, but failing to muster the courage, she insisted that the others precede her. Suddenly, it was her turn again.

She hung up there for thirty minutes, stepping tentatively to the edge several times before backing away. The sun was making a hasty descent behind the evergreens and the need to find a camp for the night was foremost in everyone's mind.

"Come on, chicken!" Frank jeered.

"You can do it, girl!" Dorothy rooted.

"You can make it, Evelyn. I know you can." John urged, professing a much stronger faith in her than she had in herself.

The others responded with similar words of encouragement, but it did no good.

Finally, with defeat clearly evident, her shaking knees buckled and Evelyn sank to the ledge in tears.

"I can't do it! I can't!" Racking sobs shook her body, her fear and frustration and utter defeat pouring out onto the ground before Michael's feet.

Feeling the warmth and security of strong arms around her, she looked up through her tear-fogged eyes at Michael staring down at her. She felt his lips touch her hair, and his hand brushed down her head and back. He was holding her, soothing her, cradling her with his big, strong body as gently and carefully as if she were a hurt child.

She listened to his commanding voice and wallowed in his calm control. "Stimmer, you and Stipple get everybody down to that creek below us. Walk about a half a mile south and make camp. We'll be there shortly."

Michael stood and watched the bedraggled hikers

make their way down into the canyon below them until he lost sight of them as they entered a thick stand of pines.

Sitting down on the ledge beside the still tearful Evelyn, Michael waited, his breath fanning against her tear- and sweat-stained cheek. He sighed, aware of a pain that came from pushing another human being too far. But then, that was his job—to push people to their limits. Still, knowing the hurt in both physical pain and bruised pride that Evelyn was experiencing did nothing to ease his conscience.

"Why don't you just leave me here?" Evelyn sobbed. "I know that's what you want to do."

"I don't want to leave you here, Evelyn. That's the last thing that would have entered my mind."

She lifted her tear-streaked face to glare at him. "I know what you want," she cried. "You want me to admit my defeat, to say you've won the war. Well, all right. You've won. Are you happy? You've won!" Again, she broke down in uncontrollable sobs. But this time, her tears did not move him to sympathize. They were forced and he knew it.

When she had recovered from her humiliating experience sufficiently, she began to reassess her ability to hold off against this man who seemed bent on conquering her. It was a frustrating assessment, to say the least. She had no more tactics, no more weaponry. Her forces of strength were depleted. She had to admit it. He had won.

"You've won, Michael." She stated it simply and quietly, wondering what effect this man's possession was going to have on her life. She could not look at him, staring instead out over the canyon, where peaceful dusk contrasted sharply with the black smoke of defeat that swirled through her mind. "I can't go on with this. You can have what you want."

She waited for his reply, then became impatient when he refused to answer. She turned to glare at him and was surprised by the laughter that fanned in tiny lines out from the corners of his blue eyes. He was watching her, waiting for something. But for what, she could not fathom.

"I said you can have what you want, damn it! Now, would you just take it and get it over with."

The deep laughter that bounded off the canyon walls and struck discordantly against her ears filled her with ominous confusion. The sound of it alone, that rich, masculine timbre, sent electrical shivers up and down her spine. But for the life of her, she couldn't decide whether they were shivers of desire or of fear.

She continued to stare at him while he laughed. Was he laughing at her? Unable to stand it any longer, she demanded an answer. "What are you laughing at?"

He sobered immediately, his eyes drilling into her. He leaned closer and his finger ran a slow trail down the inside of her thigh and back up again. "Let me tell you something about me, Evelyn. It's a quirk in my character, I suppose. But whatever it is, this fact remains. I have no intention whatsoever of taking anything from you."

"But...I thought you..."

His hand closed around her thigh, causing her mouth to clamp shut with surprise and apprehension. "I didn't say I didn't want you." His eyes slid down to her breasts and then lower to her hips and legs. "I just said I have no intention of taking it. You see...part of our bargain was that I could have it the way I wanted it. Remember?"

She nodded reluctantly, a quiet wariness sliding along her nerves and alerting every fibrous tissue of her body. "I don't understand. I..."

"I know you don't, Evelyn. You have no earthly idea what I want. But I'm going to tell you." His palm began a slow massage on her thigh, his fingers kneading the flesh, disturbing Evelyn's pulse. "You see, my love"— his voice was a whispering rush of sound, washing across her neck and face—"you are going to give me what I want. I'm not going to take it."

Startled, Evelyn could barely control the electrical jolt that jumped inside her. "I know what you want from me, Michael," she countered softly. "And I'm not sure I'm ready to give you that."

"I know you're not," he answered, sending her still moist eyes upward to stare in surprise at his gently smiling face.

"I told you the other night, I would have it when and how I want it. Well, this is not when or how I want it."

A strange flood of relief, tinged with trickles of regret washed through her. He wasn't going to force her to pay up. He wasn't going to be one of those ruthless soldiers who rape and pillage. He was simply going to take her as his prisoner of war.

"What do you want me to do then?" she asked weakly.

He smiled, a slow, victorious smile of a conqueror, of a man who knows that he has won and is ready to reap the rewards of conquest. He stood and held her hand, pulling her with him. "I want you to make this jump."

When she pulled back, fear taking hold of her once again, he grasped her arm and forced her to look at him. "I've won the right to make you do whatever I want, right?"

Nodding with begrudging reluctance, she let him lead her to the edge of the ledge.

With no effort at all, he bounded to the lower rock, then turned with an outstretched arm to help her make the jump.

It was several agonizing moments before she could face the prospect of jumping with any degree of confidence. She was truthful enough with herself to know that she could not have made it unless he had been standing there to catch her.

Bracing herself one last time, she finally leapt onto the lower rock and into Michael's waiting arms.

He held her close while she tried to still her anxious breathing and soon the sound of his heart beneath her ear and the soothing massage of his hands as they caressed her spine calmed her frazzled nerves. In their place, she felt a surging pride over the accomplishment, stronger than any she had ever felt before.

He smiled, understanding her sense of pride, knowing no words were needed to enhance that feeling. With cautious steps, he helped her down from the ledge, across the slick, lichen-covered boulders and down to the pine-needled floor of the forest. Walking through the trees, he held her close to him, his sure steps guiding her through the quiet refuge of the thicket.

Michael stopped by a rapidly flowing creek, the bubbling water rushing over the rocks, filling Evelyn's ears with its hypnotic roar. Finding a soft place in the tall grass, Michael sat down, leaving her standing before him. She cocked her head quizzically at him, wondering what he wanted now. Weren't they going to try to catch up with the other members?

Michael leaned back in the grass, resting his weight on his elbows, and watched her watching him. "Tell me again that I've won, Evelyn."

She was startled by the demand. What would he ask of her now? She had told him she wasn't ready to give him the physical payment he had won by her admission of defeat. In a way, she knew that was a lie. She would give him anything and that realization frightened her like no other. Something within her could deny him nothing. "You've won, Michael."

"What have I won?"

"You've...won...the right to...to do what you want with me."

"Not good enough." His voice was detached and even, the voice of command. The voice of a victor.

"I don't know what you want!" she cried. She was afraid now, genuinely afraid of what this man would demand of her. Not so much what he would demand of her physically, as what he wanted emotionally. What kind of commitment did he expect?

"Yes, you do know what I want, Evelyn." His voice was low and steady, his eyes penetrating the thin veneer of her emotional buttress.

She stood stock-still, afraid to move, afraid to give him that stronger than physical gift that he seemed to expect. But her will was crumbling. She could not hold out against him any longer. After all, he had won the war.

"You have..." She cleared her throat nervously and began again. "You've won... me."

"Say it again," he demanded.

Her eyes locked with his, a magnetic wave of desire capturing her in the path of that cobalt fire in his eyes, pulling everything from her. She had no will to deny him anything. "You've won me, Michael."

She watched those intense blue eyes close for one second, and the muscle in his cheek jumped. When he stood and began walking toward her, his eyes were filled with barely contained desire.

When his hands touched her waist, she felt an even greater weakening in her limbs, and her fingers clutched his wrists in an effort to remain standing.

One hand left her waist to wander upward along her side, traversing to the left to gently stroke the swell of her breast.

While his hand was given the freedom to roam at will, Evelyn's eyes never left his face. Never had a man's touch filled her with such reckless cravings. The physical side of her life had been subordinated to her career, leaving her no time for emotional attachments or for love.

"Michael." She closed her eyes, the touch of his fingers as they roamed possessively across her breasts and neck and back choking off all words, all thought. It was a totally new and thrilling experience for Evelyn to revel in pure sensation, caring nothing about the past or future. The present was all there was.

Michael brushed light kisses across her face, holding back deliberately until he felt her need reaching the height of his own. As his lips moved closer to hers, he felt her head turn, her mouth seeking the possession of his.

The languorous kiss, along with the waning light, had a drugging effect on them both, pulling them into the dusky glow of desire.

It was a slow awakening into the passion she felt for him. It was as if she were falling ever so slowly off the treadmill into Michael's arms, not caring at all that life was going to go on without her.

His moist tongue moved in deliciously slow circles around her mouth, softening her lips until they were begging for the imprint of his. Finally succumbing to her appeal, he moved his lips onto hers, molding them to fit the contour of his mouth while his hands kneaded her flesh until her supple body nestled against the configuration of his larger frame.

Evelyn could feel the pommeling of hearts, but did not know where the pounding of hers ended and his began.

Her own hands had begun a foray across his chest, over his shoulders, and into the thatch of brown hair that covered his head.

She felt a contradictory mixture of tenuity and initiative in the wanderings of her fingers as they grasped and pulled the dark strands of hair.

She wanted this man. It would be asking too much to sort out the reasons why at this moment. It was enough to know that she wanted him. And by the response of his mouth on hers and the urgently restless migration of his hands, she knew that he needed her too.

But suddenly her soaring assurance in the reciprocated passion deflated like a punctured balloon when Michael abruptly pulled away from her. She watched in bewilderment as he walked about ten feet away, raked agitated fingers through his hair, then turned and stared thunderously at her as if she had forced an unwanted sexual response from him.

Michael groaned inwardly. He hadn't meant to do that. He hadn't meant to let his physical needs get in the way of what he knew was right, what he felt he had to do for this woman and for himself. But she had been so close, so vulnerable, so touchable. It was that damn bargain that kept getting in the way. He did not want to be used. He didn't want Evelyn to get away with that. Not with him.

"You don't have to look at me like some sort of freak in a sideshow," she snapped, her nerves, still raw and sensitive from the physical stimulation, now rapidly raveling into confusing balls of twine. "If I've disappointed you in some way..." Her pride forbade her to continue any further. It was one thing to subordinate one's hidden yearnings to a career. It was quite another thing to allow those same longings free rein and then have them rejected.

Michael took a step toward her to refute what she believed to be a rejection, but Evelyn stopped him with an onrush of words. She couldn't stand the humiliation of having him smooth over the rebuff with insincere kindness.

"What about my end of the contract?" she blurted out, aware that his jaw had tightened visibly the moment she asked that question. "I mean just because you're not getting what you bargained on, does that mean you won't uphold your end?"

Michael grimaced. Vulnerable, my ass. He had been right. All she cared about was that goddamn bargain. No way was he going to let her know that he was interested in more than that either.

"I told you I would collect on it when and where I want," his voice grated harshly, the muscle in his jaw jerking as his mouth closed.

"But what about my end of it?" she forced the painful words from her lips, knowing that she had already given him so much more than he could ever imagine.

"You're still afraid of getting hurt, aren't you? Still unwilling to give up seven days of your precious schedule for something new and different." His voice and eyes were full of scorn, filling Evelyn with as much confusion as hurt. "Well, don't worry my innocent," he said scathingly. "You have my protection. For now."

Chapter Five

Though the pain of rejection persisted, it was both a physical and mental relief to Evelyn that Michael stuck to his part of the bargain. The following morning, as the rest of the group was preparing to break camp, Michael tersely informed them that Evelyn was not feeling well and would not be taking part in all of the strenuous exercises that day.

Each of the group members had his or her own private assessment of Evelyn's special treatment.

Dorothy glared at her as if this particular action of Evelyn's guaranteed the defeat of the Equal Rights Amendment.

Frank, on the other hand, was as crude as ever. "Wrong time of the month, sweetheart?" he whispered caustically in Evelyn's ear. "Or maybe old Michael has found out just how far you'll go to get what you want in life."

If that remark had come a week ago, Frank would have sported a red welt on his cheek where Evelyn would have struck it with the palm of her hand. But today, she did not slap him. She did not even respond with an indignant retort. Frank's words were too full of truth. She had made a bargain with Michael and, worse, she had been willing to carry it to fulfillment. She honestly had to admit that she would not have pulled away from him last night. She had wanted and still wanted to give him his payment due.

Something had happened to her by the creek last night. Something that had never happened with any other man before. She had given of herself. Not just her sexuality...but herself. Michael had drawn from her the very essence of her being, and he had made her want to share what Evelyn Scott was with him. She had put herself into his hands, wanting for the first time to be guided by another. But she had done it under the guise of a payment she owed to Michael. She had wanted him, and yet when he rejected her, she let him think that she was merely upholding her end of the bargain.

She knew just what he must think of her. What kind of person she was. But then, he would be right. For the first time in her life, Evelyn let the doubts linger for a while in her mind. Maybe, just maybe, she had pushed too hard, letting the end justify the means.

And perhaps she hadn't taken enough time away from her career to enjoy the simpler things that life had to offer. It was because of Michael that she could now see that. He was the one who forced her to step off the narrow path and look at her life in a new, more reflective, way. But she had used him. If she could just make it up to him, let him know that she didn't care about the bargain anymore. Ah, but she did care, that was the rub. She couldn't handle any more of the physical trauma, this endurance test, this attempt to gain confidence through stretching one's physical limitations.

No, she needed Michael. And besides, he had only tried to win Evelyn for some goal of his own. It was merely a bet with the other instructors or a private game he played with each new expedition he led into the wilds.

She couldn't humiliate herself further by letting him know that she had given more than the contract required. She would not let this man destroy the resonant fiber that had held her together for so many years. No, she would continue to play the game as she had played it all her life. After all, Evelyn Scott was supposed to be a master at playing the game.

That morning, Michael led the group farther into the High Unitas Primitive Area. It was a breathtaking experience, both literally and figuratively. They were now hiking at about ten thousand feet in elevation and the lack of oxygen sapped energy and caused migraine headaches. Evelyn wished there was some way she could avoid even this part of the program, but she knew that Michael couldn't carry her. He had at least lightened her pack considerably, taking some of the heavier items and stuffing them into his own pack.

However, she repeatedly felt the brunt of his harsh scowls at her and knew that he was still angry over her remark last night. But then, what did he expect? After all, to him it was a contract, a business deal. She had paid and would still pay if that was what he wanted, so he had no room for complaint. She was the one with the right to be bitter, for she was the one who had given more than the contract called for, and then, on top of that, was rejected.

With the lighter load on her back and the fear of some of the harsher physical tasks off her mind, Evelyn was finally able to absorb and enjoy the scenery around her. It was another beautiful day, the sunlight drifting through the trees, the aspen quaking and shimmering against the golden backdrop. She was constantly amazed at the variety and abundance of wild flowers covering the mountain slopes and, despite Michael's attitude, felt her spirits lightening the deeper into the wilderness they went.

At each rest stop, Michael took the opportunity to impart more knowledge of survival skills. Evelyn's mind was very rarely on the lessons, because her thoughts were too absorbed on the texture of his voice and the precise, but slow, movements of his hands and the shape of his thighs under the snug-fitting jeans and the...

"Are you paying attention, Evelyn?"

"Hm? Oh...yes," she lied. "You were talking about...mushrooms, yes, mushrooms."

"That was five minutes ago." Michael scowled, irritated over her lack of concentration. "We are now discussing which wild flowers are edible and which are not. You'd better listen, because you never know when you're going to need to know this."

Why was he giving her such a dire warning? Was he thinking that she might back out on the bargain and have to undergo the same treatment as the other members. No way! The isolation period began tomorrow and there was no way she was going to be alone. No sir! She had paid enough to be excluded from that. Michael would never know how much.

Michael's gaze kept swerving toward Evelyn to make sure she was listening. Why in hell didn't she pay attention to what he was saying! This whole thing was beginning to make him very uneasy. Why had he made a bargain that he couldn't keep? He hated this feeling of deception and yet—what else was there to do? The uneasiness persisted throughout the day and he couldn't shake the nagging fits of doubt that assailed him every time he looked at Evelyn.

As they continued their hike, Michael explained to the entire group the geological structure of the Rockies, and Evelyn was constantly amazed by the extent of his knowledge. Pointing out various rock formations where glaciers caused striations or polished surfaces, he encouraged the members of the group to become acutely aware of how geological history affected this terrain upon which they walked.

"You see that valley over there." They were walking along a steep ridge that curved around one side of a mountain peak. Michael pointed across the slopes and cliffs to a mountain that appeared to have had a scoop taken out of it by an ice-cream dipper. "That was formed by a glacier. Anytime you see a U-shaped valley you can be pretty sure it was formed by glaciation. V-shaped valleys, on the other hand, were formed by streams.

"During the late Jurassic period, this whole area was a part of the Sundance Sea. Look carefully at the rocks and you may find some marine deposits."

"How were these mountains formed?" Walter Green asked.

"It would take a geologist, which by the way I am not, to explain all of the complex formations in the Rockies. But there were a variety of forces that caused the uplift. Folding, volcanoes, faults, continental drift. I do know that some of these rocks date back to three-thousand million years ago."

As Michael talked, Evelyn was aware of that special tone beneath his words that spoke almost of reverence. He loved this land. Maybe that was why he seemed so much an integral part of it. Maybe to be a part of it you had to love it; and to love it, you must first be a part of it. All she knew was that, when he spoke of it, his voice was like a soft caress mingling with the wind in the pines. If only he would talk of her like that, she thought sadly. If only she could feel that kind of love, that respect.

Later, while the others practiced rappeling down a steep cliff, Evelyn sat at the top of the ridge feeling relief in every muscle of her body that she did not have to perform this task. Just the sight of the others doing it was enough to fill her with a tightening sense of fear. After her failure to make that small jump yesterday by herself, she knew she would never have been able to do this.

"Would you like to try it, Evelyn?" The others had all made it down to the ridge below and Michael was now kneeling down beside her with a strange look of hope on his face.

"You have got to be kidding!" How could he ask her such a ridiculous thing? "After what happened yesterday on the flea's leap, you really think I want to try this?"

"I thought you might."

"We had a bargain remember? I am carrying out my part, now I expect you to do the same. I don't want to do it." Her voice carried the grating harshness of her fear. Surely he wouldn't back out now and make her do these things. It would be her ultimate humiliation.

Michael's jaw tightened in anger and frustration. *Don't do this Evelyn!* he wanted to shout. *Don't do this to yourself!*

"Right, Evelyn," he sneered. "Our...bargain." His jaw clenched several times, revealing the deep-seated anger that stirred within him. "But just don't forget that I'm not through with you yet. So you're right. You'd better not tax yourself too much today. You're going to need your strength and energy with me."

At that, Michael snapped the belt around his waist, lashed the rope to a rock on the ridge, and adjusted the rope under one of his thighs, across his torso and over the opposite shoulder. Without another glance in Evelyn's direction, he descended the cliff.

She was alone with the echo of their conversation. Why had she sounded so callous? But then, why had he? He had said he wasn't through with her yet. Her eyes closed briefly as she couldn't help but wonder what was going to happen to her when he was through with her.

She felt a shiver of longing pass through her body as she thought of tonight, and then reprimanded herself for reacting to him that way. Why couldn't she hate him? He obviously had big plans for her and she, of course, was expected to go along willingly. The only problem was that she wanted to go along. She knew she was now playing a dangerous game, a game with her own heart. But she couldn't stop. She didn't want to stop. She might only have a few more days with Michael, but she was going to make the most of those days. The desperate needs inside of her gave her no other choice. For however short a time it might be, she was his.

It was ironic, she thought; how only a few days ago seven days in the wilderness seemed like a lifetime. Seven days away from the daily grind she could not bear to leave. Now those seven days were almost over, and she found herself dreading the inevitable end.

That night, after an atrocious dinner of what Michael referred to as S.O.S. and that Evelyn vaguely recognized as chipped beef on toast, the group members clustered together around the fire for one of Michael's fireside chats. With the efficiency of a squad commander, he passed out maps and instruction sheets to each person.

"As you all know, your isolation periods begin tomorrow morning." Michael sat on a log and leaned forward with his elbows resting on his knees, his hands clasped in front of him. "I know some of you are scared, and that's okay. It's all right to be afraid of something that's unfamiliar to you."

Deep inside, each of the group members were quietly trying to deal with the very fear that Michael was talking about. Each was wondering what it would be like to exist all alone in the wilderness. Would they be able to survive the solitude?

"But sometimes," Michael continued in a calm voice, "you have to know fear of something before you can understand it and come to terms with it. That's the way it is with nature. You may be apprehensive of what awaits you in the wilderness because you are not yet familiar with it.

"You have to confront the essential facts of life before you can lose your fear of them. By having no choice but to be alone with nature, you will learn to face it and learn what it has to teach without fear."

Michael glanced uneasily at Evelyn and his eyes narrowed on her in deliberation, but she did not notice. She was relishing the delicious sense of relief that flooded through her body with the knowledge that she did not have to face what the other members were going to have to do. She had bought her pardon. Though she had paid much higher stakes than she originally intended, she was happy that at least she would be free of the fear the others were now experiencing.

"What are we supposed to do for twenty-four hours out there?" one of the men asked.

"Do..." The word from Michael's lips trailed off into the pines. "What you do doesn't really matter. It's what you feel. You can occupy your time by whittling sticks or watching ants or sorting your sunflower seeds from your chocolate chips. Or you can do nothing. You can sit and stare at a rock for twenty-four hours if you want.

"Instead of doing, I'd rather see you fill your time with thought, with planning and goal-setting. Ask yourself: What are five things you would like to do before you die?"

"Die!" Charles stammered. "Did you have to use that word?"

Everyone laughed, relieving some of the pent-up tension that hovered over the entire group.

"Okay, then," Michael smiled. "How about before you turn sixty-five?"

"Well, that's bad, but it's better than thinking about de—you know what," said Charles.

"Now." Michael stood, a move that subtly switched the tone of this discussion from one of philosophy to practicality. "You each have maps, and by now you should know how to use them. At ten o'clock on Friday morning, you should start heading for Base. Chances are you will run into each other, and that's okay. If you want to work together as a team to find the camp, you may. Or, if you'd rather practice your skills on your own, you can do it that way. It doesn't matter as long as each of you participates fully in the decision-making processes. I don't want one person taking charge and leading the others in. I want each of you to use your knowledge and aggressive instincts to find your way. Understood?''

They all nodded.

''Okay, let's get some shut-eye. In the morning, I'll take two of you at a time and show you where to camp. The rest of you can sit here and wait for me.''

The group members meandered toward their bed-rolls and quickly fell into a deep slumber preparing their bodies for the two-day ordeal in solitude and the trek back to Base. Even Evelyn was exhausted, though she had not been required to do all that the others had to do. But again, she found herself unable to sleep. She kept waiting for Michael to come to her, to take from her what she so willingly wanted to give him.

Lying in her sleeping bag, she watched surreptitiously through her dark lashes as he moved about the campsite. He first checked and sorted all the equipment that he carried in his pack, then he sat down, pulled out a small notebook and began writing. She continued watching as he leaned his head back against the trunk of a tree, closed his eyes in thought, then opened them and wrote for several more minutes in the notebook.

Michael had been trying to keep busy for the last hour so he wouldn't have to think about Evelyn. But every attempt he made was futile. If he could just figure out what it was that continually drew him toward this woman even in the face of her manipulative personality. Was it because she was so much like he had once been? Was he looking beneath the surface hostility, seeing the potential and beauty that lay buried within her?

He closed his eyes and sighed. Maybe he wasn't supposed to ask why. Perhaps it was enough that he felt something special toward her. And had from the moment he met her in New York.

After closing the book and sticking it back into his pack, he hesitantly walked over to Evelyn's bedroll after first stoking the fire with the toe of his boot. He bent down and stared at her now wide-open eyes.

"Hi." He smiled gently at her. "Why aren't you asleep?"

"Should I be?"

He shrugged, wondering if he should force himself to go to his own bedroll and go to sleep. *Leave her alone, man. Don't get yourself in deeper than you already are.* "Well, it would give me the chance to play Prince Charming and kiss you awake, anyway," he answered, knowing with every minute he stayed near her he would find it more difficult to leave her alone.

"What were you writing?" She tried to change the subject away from what she knew they were both thinking. She also needed a moment to deal with the strange shift of his mood. All day he had been nothing short of surly toward her and now his voice was as soft and gentle as a playful zephyr.

"Oh, it's a journal I keep. About each of the expeditions."

"For the school or for personal reasons?"

"Personal." He smiled crookedly. "Who knows, someday I may write a book about all of this."

"Should make sexy reading," she murmured, unable to keep the tinge of sarcasm from her voice.

"Very." He sighed, trying to weigh the various courses of action in his mind. He looked at Evelyn, then glanced at his other sleeping charges. Releasing a frustrated breath, he stood, not looking at Evelyn as he spoke. "Get some sleep. Tomorrow is going to be a long day."

He walked over to his own bedroll and lay with his hands behind his head.

Evelyn was left with a peculiar feeling of deflation, of wanting something and, at the same time, being grateful that she couldn't have it.

She closed her eyes and eventually let the fatigue carry her away into slumber.

As the following morning slowly wore on, each person was taken to his own secluded spot in the wilds and left alone to think about life or to whittle or to count ants. As the last person was led away, Evelyn was left behind in the campground to wait for Michael's return.

To say that she was uneasy was a vast understatement. Her head was in constant motion, her eyes seeking out every slight noise she heard in the shrubs. Damn it! When was Michael coming back? How would he know if she had been mauled or eaten by a bear, or attacked by a tribe of wild Indians? She hoped to Heaven there weren't any Big Foot types around. Oh, she hated this! She couldn't stand to be alone out here.

When she saw him casually meandering back through

the trees toward her, relief surged through every cell of her body.

His own reaction was unceremonious and business-like. "Are you ready to go?" He stopped only long enough to survey the campsite, making sure nothing was left behind. In fact, the only personal response Evelyn felt from him was when he helped her with her pack, looping the belt in front for her. After he lifted his own onto his back, they began heading up even higher into the mountains.

It was an unspoken arrangement between them that he would be with her for the next two days, and she sighed a prayer of relief and thanks with every passing minute.

Even though it was late morning, there was a cool fog in the air and the grass was still dripping wet. As they trudged along, their pants legs were soaked above mid-calf. Everything around them was tinged in gray. The bark and leaves of trees, the sky above, the pine-laden ground below their feet, all stained with that hard, enduring color of gray.

As the fog slowly began to roll away and the temperature rose, Michael and Evelyn were protected from the sun's direct rays by the canopy of tall trees over them. But occasionally, the yellow bands of light fell across the forest floor. Ethereal light sometimes caught the tips of pine needles, causing the smaller pine trees to shine as if they were lit by an inner source of light.

Evelyn would have preferred to walk slowly and take in more of the delights the forest offered, but Michael kept a constant pace in front of her, obviously expecting her to keep up with him. The pack was again forcing her head down and she had to content herself with watching the ground as she walked rather than stare at the sky and trees above.

Once, Michael stopped abruptly and she nearly ran into the back of him. "Look," he whispered. She followed the direction of his finger and squinted her eyes trying to focus on whatever he had seen.

"What is it?" She couldn't see anything yet.

"Deer."

She looked again and where the slope of the mountain dipped to cradle the creek in the valley below, she saw a white-tailed deer moving through the high brush toward the water. It stopped, turning to stare at the two human intruders.

In that still moment, Evelyn got a glimpse of the regal power and beauty of nature's wildlife. She could only stare back at the majestic animal, her breath taken away by its quiet, dignified pose. She didn't know that Michael was watching her closely, smiling to himself over her reaction.

Startling them both, the animal suddenly pivoted. Tensing its powerful muscles, it loped into the brush, across the creek, and back up the other side of the valley. When she could see it no longer, Evelyn turned to Michael and saw the smile upon his face.

"I've never seen anything like it!" Her excited voice held a breathless quality. "It is the most beautiful thing I think I have ever seen." She became aware suddenly of the intensity in Michael's gaze, the darkening of iris and pupil that spelled only one thing—desire. His hand reached out and cupped her cheek. His fingers trailed silkily down her cheek and the side of her throat, whispering touches that incited every nerve fiber in her body. He held out his hand and, smiling, she placed her hand and her trust in his.

They walked for at least another hour, climbing over rock slides, and trying to absorb the beauty of their surroundings. She could see now why no one who came here could ever take this land for granted. It wasn't like the city, where one becomes numb to his environment. Out here the voice of nature was ever changing. The light patterns through the trees continually shifted. The terrain sometimes dropped in gradual slopes of soft meadows and at other spots plunged in sheer rocky cliffs that had been carved by the hand of time. From one perspective, these mountains contained a cruel beauty, a harshness that demanded one's absolute respect. And then, on the other hand, there was a soft sweeping symmetry that brought a sense of peace to one's soul.

Was it her surroundings or was it walking along with her hand in Michael's that gave her such a feeling of peace, of unreality? It really was too good to be true. Life wasn't like this. This was a fantasy world that would only last for a couple more days and then she would once again face the inflexible patterned life she knew so well.

They had been walking for what seemed to Evelyn to be hours. She slowed down to ease her tired legs. "Michael, can't we stop?" Her breathing was labored and the muscles in the backs of her calves and thighs were cramped.

"Let's go just a little farther." He continued to pull her along. "You're not tired are you?" he laughed.

"I fail to see the humor in that. My legs are killing me. My neck feels like it's about to break. I'm thirsty.

I'm hungry. I want to take my shoes off." And, she wanted to add, I want you to kiss me.

"Okay, we'll stop in just a few minutes."

After fifteen or twenty more long minutes of arduous climbing, the terrain finally leveled off under a thick stand of pine trees, their needles forming a soft cushioned floor upon which to walk. However, Michael was rarely content with mere walking. He was in a constant hurry and Evelyn felt herself being dragged along at his pace.

Finally, he stopped and removed his pack beside a rapidly flowing creek.

"We'll camp here," he said, dropping down into the soft swaying grasses that bordered the stream, and patting his hand on the ground for her to join him.

She removed her own pack and plopped wearily to the grass beside him, too tired to talk. Michael watched her as she lay back in the tall grass and he wondered worriedly what the outcome of all this would be.

That evening they cooked a light meal and ate in relative silence. Neither one seemed inclined to speak and, for the first time ever, Evelyn was enjoying the quiet. It was as if, with Michael, no words were needed. She remembered what he had said that first day, that sometimes the words we use mask what we're really trying to say, and she wondered if she would ever be able to shed the mask that she had worn since she was thirteen.

"Tell me about your life, Evelyn," Michael asked after dinner. They had walked to the edge of the creek and were sitting together quietly on a large boulder that contoured it.

"There's really not much to tell," she began nervously. "I have a good position with Antron...."

"Under an incompetent idiot, as I recall."

Evelyn grimaced as her own words came back to her. "I didn't really . . . I thought I was special to him. . . ."

"And because you're special, you think you shouldn't have to do the same things as other people?" Michael's arms were resting on his knees, his head cocked sideways as he watched her.

"I didn't say that," she retorted, feeling that she was being backed into a corner.

"Sometimes we demand things of other people because we care about them."

"He doesn't care about me," Evelyn's voice was soft and childlike. "I mean not really. He wouldn't have left us if he had." The stark silence that followed kept her remark hanging between them. Recoiling, she realized what she had said. Flustered, she turned her head away from Michael, hoping he would ignore the statement.

"Who left you, Evelyn?"

"No one. My father."

"When?"

"When I was thirteen."

"And you felt betrayed."

"Of course I felt betrayed," she spat out. "What are you now, my analyst?"

"I'm just a friend, Evelyn."

A friend! That's all he was, just a friend! "Well, for your information, I don't happen to arrange for casual sex with friends. And I certainly don't tell them my life history."

"Casual sex?" His hand reached out to stroke a path from the back of her head, down across her cheek and neck, following the curve of her shoulder and the long shaft of her arm. "Is that what you think making love to each other would be? Just casual sex?"

No! her heart screamed. *If you only knew how much I have already given to you, how much of my ambition and drive and future plans I have lost that will never be regained!* But she couldn't say that to Michael. She couldn't let him know how much he had won. She would never be able to live through the humiliation of seeing him gloat over his victory. It was hard enough as it was. She couldn't even imagine what it was going to be like back in New York, remembering his touch, his mouth, his hips pressed tightly against hers.

"What do you want from me, Michael?"

He watched her in silence for a long moment, while he analyzed his own intentions. "Everything you have to give," he finally answered.

Evelyn couldn't control the shiver that overtook her body. She was afraid of this man. She was afraid of what she would have to give him that he would never be able to return.

"Do you play these games with all the women you take into the wilderness?"

"I think you're forgetting, Evelyn, that it was you who made the bargain in the first place." Michael's fingers moved to the neck of her blouse and slowly and precisely began unfastening the button from its hole.

"I thought you would...I didn't expect to have to..."

"You thought you had a sucker on your hands, didn't you? One who wouldn't expect a return on his investment?" Evelyn was squirming under Michael's intense scrutiny.

"Well, let me tell you something about me, woman." He had leaned closer and his warm breath was hitting the spot between her breasts that was now exposed to him. "A long time ago, I gave up playing games. That's one of the reasons I came here to the mountains. You can't play games with nature. If you try, you will lose. And I certainly don't intend to play games with you, Evelyn."

Why did his voice, his touch fill her with such delicious yearnings? Why couldn't she just see him as a body, as a means to her end?

Michael's hands slipped under her blouse and were now roaming the softness of her skin. With the ease of his superior strength, he lifted her over to him, settling her in front of him, between the spread of his legs, her back curved against his chest. They sat there together, watching the water spill over the rocks while his hands played over the surface of her breasts and stomach and thighs.

He could feel the quivering that seized her body whenever his fingers closed around her breast. He could feel her heart beating erratically beneath his fingers. He could tell that she was deeply affected by what he was doing to her, and yet there was a rigidness to her body that still had not melted.

"I think Evelyn Scott is more innocent than she pretends to be," he whispered, tilting her head back on his shoulder.

"I'm not a virgin, if that's what you mean." Her eyes were cast in the direction of the water, away from his piercing scrutiny.

"You don't have to be a virgin to be innocent, Evelyn." His voice was so gentle next to her ear that she could not stop the liquefied warmth that fused through her bloodstream.

"I am thirty-one years old, Michael," she stressed, trying to hamper his investigation into her past.

"And you've never been in love, have you?"

"I told you, I'm not a virgin," she snapped.

"You want to talk about it?"

"No." Her face was pinched into tight lines of frustration. Feeling the profound sense of defeat under this man's penetrating stare, she sighed. "The first time I ever made love, I was twenty-four years old. Can you believe that? Twenty-four years old and still a virgin." She kept her face directed toward the stream, not wanting to know what thoughts were behind Michael's gaze.

"I had been so involved with undergraduate and graduate school that I never took the time to think much about sex. Sounds rather bizarre, doesn't it?"

Michael didn't answer, but he tensed with the pain and frustration that was slowly pouring from Evelyn.

"Then," she continued, "after I started working for Antron, I found that I was consumed with it."

"With work?"

"No," she looked away, embarrassed. "With sex. I kept wondering about what I might have missed." She paused, not knowing how to continue with this very personal history.

"And so you found someone to show you what you'd been missing," Michael prodded.

Evelyn nodded her head slowly. "I found him. He found me. I don't really know which way it was. I know I didn't love him. Oh, he was very gentle and kind, but ... Anyway, I was able to attack my work with a new zeal after that, going for long periods of time without even thinking about sex."

She sighed wearily. "I suppose I should be grateful

that the few experiences I have had were so undynamic for me, so that I could concentrate instead on my career."

"And you are not?"

"In a way; I am." She paused. "And in a way I'm very, very sorry."

Michael turned her face sideways until she was once again looking at him. His eyes were soft and understanding, without being full of pity. She was grateful for that. The one thing she had never wanted was pity. Her mother received the pity of friends and neighbors for years and Evelyn believed it had had an irreparable, debilitating effect.

"Tell me about yourself, Michael."

"What do you want to know?" His lips touched the side of her neck, his tongue blazing a slow trail up to her ear.

"Everything." Her voice had a soft, ragged sound, her breath becoming more shallow as his mouth nuzzled her neck and she felt him hardening behind her hips.

"That could take a very... long... time." His words too were beginning to flow with less ease.

She tilted her body and head back against his shoulder and left arm as his mouth moved closer to hers. He teased at the corner of her lips, his teeth catching her lower one between his. Then his tongue began a slow outline of her now parted mouth.

He pulled his head back slowly and smiled into her eyes. "What do you want to know, Evelyn?" His voice was nothing more than a seductive whisper, filling her with the most intense craving she had ever known.

Everything! she wanted to say. *I want to learn every-*

thing you can teach me. Her lips were parted and the words almost escaped, but the overwhelming fear of rejection kept her from surrendering to him. She couldn't let him overpower her again. He could very easily reject her in the same callous manner he had used before.

She forced her thoughts away from what she knew they both wanted her to say. "What did you do before you came to the mountains?" she asked instead in a tremulous voice.

Michael expelled a slow breath and smiled, but it was a wistful smile. "My parents died when I was seventeen, and during my later school years I lived with a good friend of the family. In sixty-five I was sent to Vietnam." He paused, trying to decide how many memories of that time to share with her.

"After the war, I drifted for several years, moving from place to place, job to job. Dissatisfied is the operative word here. I was disillusioned by what happened in the war and I couldn't find any direction in my life. Then, I came to Utah and landed a job as ski instructor. I grew up in Vermont, so I had skied all my life."

Michael sat quietly, his thoughts private and introspective.

"Didn't you have anything else you could fall back on... something else?"

Michael's attention was drawn back to Evelyn and he stared at her for a long moment, once again deliberating how much he should tell her. "Look, Evelyn," he chuckled. "I know you're afflicted with that old puritan work ethic, but..."

Evelyn looked uncomfortable. "I just thought that

maybe you had some skill...or training in something other than..."

"Oh, I get it." He was laughing harder now, making Evelyn feel even more uncomfortable. "Evelyn Scott is not sure she should be associating with someone who doesn't have more on the ball than to be a ski or wilderness instructor, right?"

"That's not true!" She was perfectly indignant over such a suggestion. "I just—"

"It is true." He pointed an accusing finger at her, though his face retained a hint of amusement. "You're a snob."

"What? I most certainly am not a snob!"

"Evelyn Scott is a class-A snob." He held her face up where she was forced to look at him.

"I'm not!"

"You are!"

"I'm not a..." She sighed, realizing she was defeated. And perhaps he was right. She was snobbish, giving more importance to what a person did for a living than what he was as a person. "I'm sorry, Michael." She was disgusted with herself for being the way she was and yet she wondered if she would ever, could ever, change.

Michael smiled gently and brushed her hair back from her face. "Hey, would it make you feel better if I said I was a lawyer or something?"

She shrugged her shoulders as if she didn't care.

"Okay, I'm a lawyer. How's that?" He kissed her forehead lightly. "Now, does that make you feel better?"

"Where did you learn to make love?"

"Ah-ha! Now we're getting down to what the lady really wants to know," he laughed.

"I'm serious." She turned around on his lap until she was facing him and playfully struck his chest.

His hand began a slow foray over her back, down her side, stopping to rest on her hipbone. "First of all, I have to take issue with your terminology. I learned the fundamentals of having sex a long time ago. But making love...well"—his fingers squeezed the flesh of her thighs—"that's something that only happens between certain people." His breath touched her temple before his mouth brushed across the skin.

Believe it, Evelyn. You can believe whatever you want. Was he talking about the two of them? Was he saying that he was feeling the same crazy emotions she was?

Evelyn's eyes locked with Michael's and she saw a reflection of her own wants and needs. They both stared, unable to tear their eyes away from each other. Michael reached up with his hands, running his fingertips down the sides of her face, the outline of her jaw and nose. Finally, the pressure increased slightly as he pulled her face nearer.

Their mouths moved closer, almost touching, one pair of lips brushing lightly on the other—never embracing, yet opening and closing as they barely made contact, hinting at the sensual delight to come.

Without a word, Michael turned her so that she could be lifted, bent a forearm behind her knees and another arm beneath her shoulders, and lifted her up and carried her down from the rock and onto a soft grassy bed by the creek.

As he walked and held her in his arms, Evelyn pressed her lips into his neck, tasting the slightly salty taste of his skin. Michael's mouth dipped down to the soft mounds of her breasts, a worshiping caress that filled her with an inexpressible sense of belonging to this man.

He set her body gently in the grass and lay down beside her, easing his knee between her legs. His hands were in her hair and his mouth moved slowly from her throat across her chest, kissing the skin that was exposed at the neckline of her shirt—whispering touches that were as fresh and moist as dew drops on the columbine flowers that surrounded them.

They did not speak, for neither felt the need for words. The sounds of nature around them spoke more eloquently than either of them could have.

Grasping her hips with one hand and her back with the other, Michael rolled over, pulling Evelyn atop him. Now her lips played across his forehead and cheeks and throat and chest, teasing sips that stoked the blazing fire within him.

Straddling his hips, she sat up, and never removing her gaze from his she slowly unbuttoned the second button of her chambray shirt. Pulling the hem from beneath the waistband of her corduroy jeans, she lifted the blouse over her head.

As the bottom of the shirt moved up her torso and over her head, Michael sat up, holding her in his lap, and wrapping his arms around her back, his mouth took advantage of the soft skin now exposed to him. He kissed and tasted her breasts, never taking his mouth away from her skin as he moved from one to the other. He heard the soft moan that Evelyn could not contain as she quickly pulled the shirt all the way off, then she tilted her head back, arching her body toward Michael's mouth.

With a low groan, he rolled her back over and lay

atop her, his mouth and hands moving with anxious need across her body.

Evelyn was subliminally aware of the wind blowing through the trees above them, and the occasional mating call of a bird punctuated her own sighs of ecstasy.

Michael skillfully removed her jeans and his own clothes, and after he sighed her name softly and lovingly, together their bodies swam in a fragrant sea of fertile wild flowers, languorous, caressing breezes, and untamed passion.

Michael's hands nourished her body the way the rain fed the forest floor. And the water in the creek flowed swiftly downstream, whirling jets of melted snow that played and danced over the rocks, gurgling to the tune of their absolute fulfillment.

Chapter Six

As first light swept over the pine trees and the dew began to burn off the knee-deep grasses, six weary people were at last understanding the difference between the raw, elemental wilderness and the corporate jungle.

They had been alone for twenty-four hours, some of them thinking of their lives and the directions they wanted to take in their remaining years, others sorting through their high-energy snacks or watching insects. But all were giving their minds a much needed rest from the continual stream of plans and projects, accounts and clients. In different ways, they all felt renewed.

As mid-morning approached, they began moving down the mountain, trying to utilize the skills they had been learning for the last week. As Michael had predicted, some of them found themselves on the same path, joining forces for their journey back to camp, while others had to make their own way.

At this same time, Evelyn was finding her own sense of renewal. She was enjoying the security of Michael's calm command, her thoughts far removed from the problems of a week ago, when every waking moment was trained on success, no matter what the price. And, too, she now knew that she was in love with this man. As wrong as he was for her life and she was for his, there was no denying what she felt for him.

While it was still early morning, and the cool silence lingered in the grass, Evelyn and Michael systematically cleaned up their campsite, storing their supplies in the packs, and sharing a quiet bond of communion with nature and with each other.

Michael was using the toe of his boot to kick dirt onto the last remaining embers of their fire, following a pattern that had become second nature to him over the last few years. But his thoughts were troubled. He kept picturing Evelyn's eyes last night when he held her. She had been so trusting, so vulnerable in that moment.

Although from the moment he first met Evelyn, he had wanted to make love to her, he never meant for things to turn out this way. When she made the bargain with him that first night in camp, he had played along with it only to frighten her into performing rather than to actually hold her to it.

Now he had gone too far. If damage had been done, he could not now undo it. Even now, when he thought of her softness, her response to him, he had to fight every muscle in his body to keep from reaching out and touching her again. But what would she think of him after today? Would she feel that she had been betrayed?

He kicked the dirt harder than necessary with his boot as he tried to shove away the guilt.

"Do you trust me, Evelyn?" Michael's forehead was drawn into a frown as he began to tie his sleeping bag to the pack frame.

Startled over his question, her head jerked up. "Shouldn't I?" she asked warily, her voice sending short clouds of vapor into the morning air.

"Yes," he answered slowly, picking and choosing his words very carefully. "Yes, you should. I just want you to know that I would never do anything to hurt you."

Now it was Evelyn's turn to frown. She continued to clean up the campground, but a slim shadow of foreboding accompanied her every movement. What was he worried about, she wondered, and should she perhaps be worrying too?

When the last of the equipment was finally loaded into their packs, they set out through the trees for the trip back to Base Camp. It was going to be a long hike. One or two days anyway, and Evelyn wasn't looking forward to it at all. She turned around once to look back at their peaceful spot by the creek, and a chord of sadness struck inside her chest at the thought of leaving it.

As they walked, Michael and Evelyn talked about the different routes the team members might take and the types of problems they might run into. He insisted, as he had several times before, that the school had never lost a student—not yet, anyway. Evelyn was constantly aware that Michael seemed distracted this morning and absorbed by some deep thoughts of his own so, as much as possible, she left him alone, figuring that if he wanted to talk he would.

She began thinking about how differently things had turned out from what she had expected. Six days ago, she had arrived in Utah full of fear and anger, unable to accept this seven-day disruption of her schedule, worried over whether she would survive the physical trauma of this experience, and damning Michael every step of the way for tricking her boss into sending her here. Seven days had then seemed a lifetime.

It was true, though; the first two days had been pure hell and she had constantly felt emotionally drained from the war she was then waging with Michael. But now, everything seemed so beautiful. He wasn't at all the type of man to whom she was accustomed. Yet she had found a sense of peace with him that she had never known before.

She had always been alone. Fending for herself. It was nice—very nice—to let this man take care of her for a while. She was afraid this all might end in a day or two, but she had to be realistic. This was his life, while hers was in New York City. In a week's time, this could all be nothing more than a memory, fading rapidly beneath the kinetic brilliance of her everyday life.

She sighed heavily, knowing how distorted her rationale was. This was one memory that would never fade.

She glanced at Michael, feeling a tinge of annoyance that he was so distant this morning.

"Is everything okay?" she asked tentatively, knowing that something was definitely bothering him. "You don't think any of the others are lost, do you?"

Michael scanned the horizon as if he could see each of his students. "No...no, I'm sure everyone's okay."

"Well, is something the matter?" she tried again.

"No," he answered much too quickly and curtly. "Nothing's the matter." He turned away from her and continued hiking. She watched him with confusion. Had she done something? Said something that might have provoked this attack of moodiness?

She held back any further comments or questions and just kept her eyes on the back of his strong legs as they moved with the ease and grace of a mountain lion over the uneven terrain. She occasionally studied the landscape and the raw beauty that surrounded them in every step. But mostly she watched Michael, still afraid that if she turned away, she would lose sight of him and be lost in this wilderness forever.

It was in one of those rare moments when she took her eyes off of him that it happened. She had paused to admire a purple wild flower and suddenly felt the hair rise on the back of her neck. Something was wrong. When she raised her eyes again toward Michael, his feet slipped on some loose rocks. He began tumbling, rolling, as if in slow motion, over and over again down the steep, rocky slope.

"Michael!" Evelyn jumped up, tripping and stumbling over the uneven ground, and began running as fast as she could with the heavy pack on her back. When she got to the top of the slope and looked down, she saw that Michael had stopped falling. He was lying on his back, one knee raised, and he was not moving. Evelyn thought she heard a groan. She sat down and began sliding down the hill on her bottom, using her hands and heels to hug the slope and to keep her body from moving too fast.

"Michael!" she screamed as she reached him. Kneeling down beside him, she grasped his hand. His eyes were open and he was looking at her, but he seemed to be in a great deal of pain. His foot and leg appeared to be wedged under a large boulder, so she tried to get into a position to push the rock away.

"No!" Michael lifted his head and reached out and clasped her wrist. "No!" His breath was ragged with pain and that one word seemed to expend all of his energy. He dropped his head back to the ground and closed his eyes briefly. "Don't move it."

"Okay." Evelyn was near tears. What could she do to help him? She quickly grabbed one of the canteens, opened the cap, and poured a small amount of water into his mouth. Michael smiled weakly. "What do I do, Michael? Are you in a lot of pain? Tell me what to do?" Her voice was reaching almost hysterical proportions.

"First, you've got to relax, Evelyn. Everything's going to be... okay." He choked as if the act of speaking were causing him even greater pain. He picked up his radio transmitter and tried to contact Base. There was only dead air space. He tried again but still received no answer, the silence almost deafening to Evelyn's ears. "It's broken." He looked at her for a long moment, thinking of the best way to tell her. "You've got to get help, Evelyn. You've got to get to Base and get help."

"Base!" She lifted her head and looked about in agitation, trying to get her bearings. "I...I don't know where it is. I don't know how to find it!"

"You'll have to... listen to me for a minute. I'll explain..."

"I can't do it, Michael! I can't find my way by myself. You can't ask me to do that. You can't!"

"Evelyn!" Michael grabbed her upper arm and squeezed it painfully. "Get hold of yourself. Now!"

She stared at him in bewilderment for a moment and then began to cry. Michael began to stroke her hair, but his arm dropped to the ground wearily.

"Evelyn, remember how you reacted the other day on the Flea's Leap?" His voice was intense. He had to make her understand that she could do it.

"I remember." Evelyn was still crying. "But this is different, Michael. I don't know what to do. I don't even know where to begin."

"Of course you do. I've taught you the skills you need to know."

"But I didn't pay enough attention. I thought...I planned on..."

"What are you going to do, Evelyn? Nothing?" His voice was slow and tinged with frustration. "Would you just let me die here?"

"Of course not!" she gasped, staring at his trapped leg, every ounce of energy within her trained on willing the boulder to move. Here was the man she had thought could protect her. The only man in whom she had ever put her trust. Now, he was putting his trust in her.

They both remained silent for several soul-searching seconds. Finally, Evelyn spoke, but her voice was nothing more than a frail whisper.

"Tell me what to do, Michael." She saw him open his eyes slowly and noticed that the spark of confidence had returned in them.

Michael spent the next few minutes helping her to get her bearings and pointing her in the direction of Base Camp. He briefly summarized instructions he had given the entire group for the last six days, quickly reviewing the basics of the compass, map interpretation, and mountain survival.

His voice droned on with tips and instructions, while Evelyn sat paralyzed with fear. But at least this time she did listen.

After he had finished the instructions, he admonished her to stop at night and sleep, informing her that it would probably take her about two full days to get there.

When he finished speaking, he lay there watching her intently. He was trying to decide if she could do it, if she had listened to him at all. Slowly, she began to nod.

"All right," she said softly. "I guess..." She looked around fearfully. "I guess I'd better go." Looking back at Michael, she touched his arm gently. "Will you be all right?"

He nodded. "You take care of yourself, okay? Do just what I told you and you'll be fine too."

"I know." She didn't know, but she thought it best not to worry him too much. She felt a sudden urge to kiss him, and as she leaned over his mouth she was startled by his reaction. He reached his arm around her pulling her down against his pounding chest and his mouth opened onto hers with almost feverish desire.

Breathless, she pulled away from him and reluctantly stood to go. "Here's your canteen and—oh, here, let me get a blanket for you.... Oh no! I just thought of something. How am I going to tell them where to find you?"

"Just tell Josh that I'm near that old mine shaft we found last month. He'll know what I mean."

Evelyn nodded her head slowly. "All right." She loaded her pack onto her back, this time correctly fastening the strap around her waist. "I'll be back, Michael." Evelyn turned quickly and hurried away before he noticed that she was beginning to cry. Heading down the slope, she had to grasp at rocks and trees to keep from falling the way Michael had done.

She had no idea where she was going other than in

the direction Michael had started her. She stopped and
looked at her compass. Southwest. That was the way
Michael had said to go. Base Camp was southwest of
her present location. Okay, she would try to keep on
that course. She looked up behind her at the sun. It was
climbing steadily in the eastern sky and was almost at
the midway point. That would only give her about eight
more hours of daylight. Eight more hours! How in
God's name was she going to make it for eight hours by
herself? All she wanted was to sit down and cry. Maybe
she needed a short nap. No! She had to get help for
Michael. Michael was lying there in agony. If anything
happened to him . . . No, she had to keep going. She had
to keep putting one foot in front of the other, for each
step brought her that much closer to the camp and help
for Michael.

She crossed a grassy meadow before entering a thick
stand of aspen trees. As she continued to climb, the
aspen gave way to dense groves of pine and spruce.
She threaded her way across a rocky ridge along one of
the buttes, then slowly began descending again to the
valley below.

Her legs felt like rubber that had been stretched tightly
to the snapping point. Her back ached from the weight of
the heavy pack. Her shoes were so worn and thin by now
that she felt almost as if she were walking on the blisters
of her bare feet. As she forced herself to keep walking,
she didn't realize that she had begun to cry again. The
tears fell silently on her cheeks and onto her shirt. Had
she even known they were there, she wouldn't have had
the strength to lift her arm to wipe them away.

She followed the southwesterly course for two or
three more hours, stopping every few minutes to check

her compass heading and rest her aching legs and back. But she quickly realized that the rest periods were filled with anything but rest.

She jumped at every sound in the brush, grew nauseated at the sight of a vulture circling lazily above her, and shivered every time her exhausted mind and distorted rationale visualized a bear or cougar lurking behind the trees.

It was better to keep walking and not think too much. She would just place one leaden foot in front of the other and concentrate on Michael's instructions.

When she became hungry, she stopped, released her pack to the ground behind her and pulled out a piece of beef jerky and some dried apricots. Immediately readjusting the pack on her back and chewing mechanically as she walked, she continued on her route. By now, concentration was becoming more difficult. She kept thinking of Michael lying there in pain. Kept visualizing vultures circling slowly, patiently waiting, above his trapped body. Her mind began to play tricks on her. She would visualize him lying there in agony and the next minute she would be on top of him, the two of them rolling down the hill while they made love. In her mind, she could feel his hands on her body, but in her next thought his skin was cold and lifeless.

Evelyn screamed as she lost her footing. Tumbling down a steep slope, she grabbed at passing rocks and trees to stop her. Finally hitting the wide, rough trunk of a spruce, she stopped, her body numb and still. She lay that way for several minutes, stunned, until she heard a thrashing on the hill behind her.

She glanced up, but her eyes were so blurry, she could only see the outline of something or someone running toward her. A bear! It had to be a bear coming after her! She forced her sore body up and began moving down the hill at a pace only slightly slower than a run. She had to get away from the animal. She had to get away!

When she no longer heard the charging figure behind her, she slowed her pace a bit. She kept moving, up and down and around, following the vague pointing of a magnetic needle. She plunged down a slope into a V-shaped valley. What had Michael said about V-shaped valleys? Why couldn't her brain seem to remember anything? Oh yes, water! A V-shaped valley was formed by water. There must be a stream somewhere around here. She walked through the valley, wading high grasses and marshes until she found a small stream. She checked the ground around it. It was soft, but well hidden in the grass. She would sleep here. There would be water, protection; it was as good a place as any.

About thirty feet from the spot she had chosen the stream flowed into a log-jammed beaver pond. All around, the mountains towered over her, isolating her from the world beyond. She was alone. Alone with the rapid beating of her heart and her tired, aching body. The wind swept the loneliness around her. She lay down in the grasses, her head resting on her pack. Maybe just a short nap, a little rest was all ...

When she awakened, the sun was only a lingering glow on the western horizon. She sat up, at first confused as to where she was. Where was Michael? Why wasn't he with her? She looked around frantically before remembering. Oh, yes, he was hurt somewhere up there. . . . She searched the mountain peaks around her, trying to remember in which one she had left him. Sighing, she gave up. Josh would know. Josh would be able to help her.

She pulled her pack around in front of her and began searching through it for something to eat. She untied her bedroll from the bottom, and rolled it out flat on the ground. A fire, that's what she needed. But it sounded like too much trouble. Sighing, she stood and walked over to a stand of trees where dead twigs and bark covered the ground. Loading her arms, she headed back to her spot on the creek. Hauling some rocks from the edge of the stream, she made a circle, clearing out all the grass inside.

She had watched Michael several times and hoped now that she could build one the same way he had. She began forming some small twigs into the shape of a tepee, gradually adding larger twigs as the pyramid grew. Finding her tin of matches in her pack, she struck one, only to have it immediately blown out by the wind. The next one she cupped in her hands, but by the time she touched the twigs with the match, it too had flickered out. Damn! She began to curse and throw things. *Calm down, Evelyn. Just calm down and try again.* Oh, God, now she was beginning to sound like Michael. But he was right. She was too easily excitable, too quick to give up at the first sign of trouble.

Breathing deeply to calm herself, she once again lit a match under the cover of her hands. When she touched the twigs, they caught, a tiny flame traveling down the length of the stick, its spark catching the next one on fire. She did it! It started! She slowly began to add large sticks to the fire until she had a sizable blaze. It wasn't cold yet, but it would be nice to have a hot meal. Besides, maybe it would keep away any wild animals. At the thought of what might be lurking out there in the ink-black night, she shivered and moved closer to the fire.

How did this happen? Why did it happen? Only this morning, she had been so happy about the way things had turned out. So secure in the knowledge that Michael would take care of her until she could return to her own secure and familiar world of the city. Now, all that had changed.

"Why, Michael? Why?" she cried into the air. "No." She wasn't going to get hysterical. She wasn't going to break down and cry. She wasn't! The tears fell anyway. Tears of self-pity and fear and loneliness welled up within her, rendering her incapable of all rational thought.

When she finally uncovered her eyes, she realized with dismay that the fire had gone out. She blew on the ashes, hoping to stoke up any embers that might still be aglow. Nothing. Wearily, she pulled out her metal matchbox and noticed there were only two left. She carefully lit one of them, but it blew out before the kindling could catch fire. Dejected and thoroughly frustrated, she closed the lid on the matchbox and stored it in her pack. There was only one match left. She would not use it. It would be better to tell herself that she didn't want a fire than to use her last match failing to start one.

Rummaging through her pack in the dark, she located a packet of beef jerky and began chewing methodically on the tough pieces of meat that tasted exactly like leather. How anyone could actually choose to eat this stuff was beyond her. It was horrible! She then sorted through her high-energy snacks, dividing up what she would need tomorrow and slowly eating the rest. She knew by the feel that there were still several handfuls of M&M's, two packets of sunflower seeds, a plastic bag of dried fruit, two packets of meat that would be practically inedible without a fire to cook them on, and a canteen full of water. She would refill it tomorrow with fresh water from the stream. Damn! She suddenly remembered what Michael had said the first day of hiking about sheep grazing along the streams. Oh, to hell with it! She didn't even care anymore. That day seemed so far away, an event that happened in another lifetime. She had been so concerned that day about not breaking a fingernail. Now she was worried if she would make it back to the camp alive.

As she munched on her food, she began thinking about the suggestions Michael had given the other members before they went into their isolation periods. What was it he had said? Think of five things you'd like to accomplish before you die. She guessed there wasn't much point in worrying about it if she were going to die tomorrow. But suppose she did make it? What were five things she wanted to do before she died?

She lay back on her sleeping bag, folding her hands behind her head, and watched the stars that filled the sky above her. She had always tried to force self-reflection out of her thoughts before, concentrating instead on one thing only—success. Everything she had done for the past few years had been centered around her success. Succeed, get ahead, rise to the top. Don't think about a personal life. Don't think about tomorrow. Or the day after.

The image of Michael drifted into her conscious

mind. His mouth, his hands, his smile, each separate entity that blended into a whole. She wanted to touch him, to feel his body so warm and loving next to hers. It was strange to think that they were both lying out in the wilderness alone, miles apart and yet somehow not far apart at all. "I'll get help for you, Michael." She whispered the words into the night, hoping that he would somehow hear, would somehow know how she felt about him. She gradually let the peace of the night and the closeness of their spirits envelop her in sleep.

When the early morning sounds of nature awakened Evelyn, she lay still, frozen for one long paralyzing moment until she realized where she was and what she had to do. Her muscles ached from the tedious hiking she did yesterday and she wondered if she would be able to move at all.

Slowly sitting up in her bedroll and easing her muscles into action, she reloaded her gear and began the long trek toward Camp. By mid-morning, she had to stop and remove her pack so that she could take off her cardigan sweater, then lifted the pack back on and retied it around her waist. Every action drained her of energy and she knew she had to reserve as much as possible for the remainder of the trip.

Her mind continuously reverted to Michael lying on the side of a mountain with his leg wedged painfully under a large boulder. How could it have happened? Why did it happen? She shook her head to dispel the nagging questions from her mind. She had to keep her thoughts directed on one thing—getting back to the camp and getting help for Michael.

She stopped as little as possible, setting new goals for

herself constantly. A tree, a ridge, a shadow—all goals that she could achieve, each one spurring her on to the next.

Stopping only when she absolutely could go no farther, she felt that she was making good time. If she was hungry, she would chew on a piece of jerky or munch on tiny chocolates as she walked, trying to keep her pace as constant as possible, trying to reach that next seemingly unreachable goal.

As Michael had instructed her to do, she attempted to follow the creek as it zigzagged down the valley, where it seemed to disappear at times as it narrowed down to a trickle, only to reappear a few hundred yards later in a rapid flow. Other streams and underground springs, it seemed, were filtering into this one creek and the farther down the mountain she went, the faster the creek flowed and the wider it grew. The excitement of this discovery alone gave Evelyn a new burst of energy.

Finally, in the late afternoon, when she had just about given up hope of reaching Base before the sun made its rapid descent beyond the horizon, she stood on a ridge jutting out from the side of a slope and she saw a thin column of smoke rising from the valley below her. Checking and rechecking her map, she knew it had to be the camp. She tried to throw her arms in the air and leap for joy, but her exhausted body did not move. All she could do was smile and know that in a few hours a search party would be heading out to bring Michael home.

A light rain shower began and she relished the coolness of it against her skin and the fresh fragrance of it in the air. This new awareness of her environment, this new feeling of belonging, did not strike her with any sudden force. It simply evolved within her as she continued to move forward through the mountains. She was no longer afraid. It had nothing to do with knowing she was almost home, for the fear had been losing ground with her for hours. Something had happened within her. As she looked around her, she no longer saw a hostile environment, nor did she feel that she was an outsider. She was no longer afraid.

She looked back in the direction from which she had come. Towering pine, spiraling spruce, and stands of aspen thrust upward from the granite crust, overpowering in their somber masses. As far as she could see was an infinity of trees and flowers and water and uncompromising beauty. A panorama that demanded her deepest respect. How far she had come in seven short days!

As she rested for a moment and feasted her eyes on the magnificent scenery, a worried frown began to crease her brow. Looking back at the rise over which she had come yesterday, she became aware of a grayish-white cloud fanning and billowing out from behind the trees. Her heart felt as if it had stopped and then catapulted out of her body as she realized what she was seeing. Oh, my God! Michael was up there! It was smoke. A forest fire!

As the fear for Michael began to clutch her throat, she frantically tried to think of what to do. Panic consumed her mind for several minutes, paralyzing her in its grip. There was nothing she could do and the helplessness of the situation burned like flames inside of her. Attempting to hold the panic at bay, she turned toward Base and as quickly as possible began making her descent into Immigration Canyon. She had to hurry. Had to get there and warn everyone. Had to let them know that Michael might be trapped up there where the fire was. The rain was pouring down now, drenching her and slowing her progress, but she only hoped and prayed that it was raining as hard where Michael was.

She continued to push forward, running wherever the terrain and her aching legs allowed. She had to hurry to reach Camp. She was almost there. She had to keep going.

After an hour of the most arduous hiking she had ever imagined, Evelyn was within a hundred yards of Base Camp. At the end, she was thrashing through the trees, tearing her pants on the knee-high brush, and gasping for breath as she tried to get there quickly and get help for Michael.

When she finally stepped through the edge of the trees, into the clearing where the cabins and lodge sat, she stopped. The scene in front of her was bizarre in its domestic peacefulness. Everything was in place, people milling about casually. She could see some of her team members were already there and were sitting on the porch of the lodge laughing and sipping drinks. Smoke curled lazily out of the chimney and she could hear muffled conversations and laughter floating over to the spot where she was standing.

But the peaceful setting was not what made her stop and stare. What she saw froze the blood in her veins and brought a screeching halt to her pounding pulse. Was it a mirage? No, this was no mirage, no vision. Michael Baylor was standing there, watching her as intently as she was watching him.

She opened her mouth to say something, but let it

close again. At that moment, the shrill and piercing scream of a bluejay filled the air, making the exact sound that Evelyn would have made had her throat not been so clogged with rage.

She blinked her eyes rapidly to make sure her sight wasn't playing tricks on her. But no, it was definitely he. It was Michael standing there, leaning against the railing. He was standing by himself, away from the others, and on his face was a strange, hesitant expression. He looked cautious, afraid to move, as if he were waiting for something. And then it suddenly came to her what emotion was holding his features in that curious expression. It was a look of guilt. Plain and simple, he was guilty.

She thought she had experienced every kind of fear there was this past week. But suddenly she knew that wasn't true. There was a new kind building up inside of her. A twisted mixture of fear and hurt and rage that began to grow and expand and burn through her, tearing at what little was left of the thin fabric of her control.

They stood this way, twenty feet apart and staring, for several agonizing minutes. Finally, Michael moved slowly toward her. As tired as she was, she was standing stiffly, every muscle in her body tensed for what was about to happen. Standing only a foot in front of her, he reached out to touch her, but she jerked away as if she were about to be struck by a poisonous snake.

"Don't touch me," she hissed hysterically.

"Evelyn, let me explain." Michael's eyebrows were pulled together in a painful frown, and his hand once more reached out to her. But again, he had to pull his hand back to his side without touching her.

"Explain!" She looked over his body, his healthy, unhurt body. He had not limped over to her. He had walked, his body massed with radiating power and sturdy bones. "Explain?" Her voice had raised an octave.

"Evelyn, I had to do it. I—"

"You tricked me!" she screamed. "You lied to me and you tricked me!"

"I had to!"

"You goddamn son of a—"

"For God's sake, it's my job!" Michael tried to reach for her. "This is what I do!"

"What you do!" she literally screamed at him. "Your job! And what about the things we did the night before last," she whispered venomously. "Was that part of your job too?"

"Evelyn, stop it!" Michael grasped her wrists as they were about to strike his face, clamping his fingers tightly around her small bones. She glanced around and noticed that everyone was listening, watching with intense curiosity. She glared back at Michael and tried to rip her arms out of his grasp.

"You can let go of me now," she snarled through clenched teeth. "I won't embarrass you in front of all your friends." He released her wrists and she jerked them back to her side. "But let me tell you something, Michael Baylor," she spat the words out at him. "I am leaving this godforsaken place tonight. Right now. And I don't ever—*ever* want to speak to you, see you, hear you, or think of you again as long as I live. The war is over."

Chapter Seven

"Give me a break, Bill. I need those two acres." Evelyn covered her forehead with the hand that was not holding the telephone receiver, and methodically massaged her temples as she listened to the voice at the other end of the line droning on. When was this frightening sensation that she was hanging in limbo over some yawning abyss going to go away? It was over. The war was at an end. So why on earth did she feel the need to repeat that to herself again and again?

"Yes, Bill, I understand completely. Just do me a favor, okay? Talk to the owner again. Wine him, dine him. Do whatever you have to do to get him to sign over that lease."

As soon as she replaced the telephone receiver, Evelyn opened one of her desk drawers and extracted a bottle of aspirin. After dumping two tiny white pills into her hand, she poured a glass of water from the crystal pitcher that sat on top of the walnut credenza behind her. As she tilted her head to swallow the pills, she glanced up to see Lloyd's disapproving frown as he walked into her office.

"Another headache, Evelyn? That's the third time this week I've seen you downing pills of some sort."

"They're aspirin, that's all," she answered defensively. "And if I could get those bullheaded ranchers in North Dakota to give us permission to drill, I'd stop having these damn headaches."

Lloyd pursed his lips in disbelief. "It seems to me that if you'd stop worrying about it and slow down a bit, you'd feel just fine. You really have been working too hard lately, Evelyn. I know, I know," he said, holding up his hands in surrender when she started to interrupt. "You don't want to hear it. But it's true. You are taking on too much work and have been ever since you returned from Utah six months ago."

"Lloyd, please," Evelyn heaved a sigh of irritation. "If I thought I were doing too much, I would stop. But I'm not, so please just—" She stopped herself short of telling him to get off her back. She had been hearing these lectures from him for several months now. He was more like an old mother hen than a major corporation president, and she didn't want anyone, including her boss, trespassing into her emotional territory.

Aware that Lloyd was watching her closely, Evelyn picked up an unlit cigarette, swiveled her chair around and stared out the office window. Two days ago was the first heavy snowfall of the year and already it had turned to brown sludge on the streets and sidewalks. The colorless sky hung like a heavy layer of ashen gloom over the city and pedestrians blended into one continuous band of surly frowns. The foul mood of the weather was perfectly interwoven with Evelyn's own state of mind.

She twiddled the cigarette between her fingers, knowing she wouldn't light it, but needing the familiar distraction to keep her hands occupied.

It was true. She had been working especially hard the last few months. And her production level was at an incredible high. She was achieving the success in business transactions that she had always dreamed of and worked toward. But the feeling of satisfaction that was supposed to come with success was missing. Everything she had ever worked for now seemed tinged in the same gray as the winter sky. There was no sense of pride, no thrill of excitement, no joy of success.

She knew now—since that week in Utah—that there was something more to life than this. She still couldn't pinpoint exactly what that something was, but she couldn't deny that it was there all the same.

It was a sense of self-worth, she supposed. A feeling of being independent and dependent at the same time. Out there, she had been totally dependent on the land and yet she had merged with it, coming away with a sense of interconnectedness, of belonging, and with a new confidence in her own physical abilities.

She frowned slightly as her thoughts shifted to Michael and his treachery. She tried, as much as possible, not to think about him at all. Whenever she would relive the physical experiences of the week, she would make sure that when she painted the scenes in her mind, the canvas was devoid of his presence. She could not think about him without burning up inside with anger and hurt and unwanted longings. She hated the man and she was determined that she would wash him from her mind if it took twenty hours of work a day. Somehow she would forget him!

"What you need is a break," Lloyd said, forcing her attention away from thoughts of Michael. "Why don't you have lunch with us today, Evelyn?"

She swiveled back around to face him. "Us?" she asked distractedly, a portion of her mind still holding on to those isolated moments of greatness in Utah.

"Yes, remember I told you that—" At that moment, Evelyn's intercom buzzed. Lloyd's secretary interrupted his disclosure and informed him that his godson was waiting in his office.

"Great!" cried Lloyd. "He's here. Are you going with us, Evelyn?"

"What? Oh, no," she answered remotely. "I'm having lunch with a client today, but thanks anyway."

"Well, what about tonight?" he insisted.

The last thing she wanted to do was spend the evening with Lloyd and his incomparable godson. "No," she answered, trying to keep the relief out of her voice. "Tom Bridgestone asked me to join him at Carmello's for dinner." She was looking directly at Lloyd when she spoke, so she didn't fail to notice the expression of displeasure that crossed his face.

"Tom Bridgestone?" he murmured distastefully. "Hm," he added with a scowl.

"What's the matter, don't you approve?" Evelyn asked, half-jokingly, half in irritation.

"Tom Bridgestone is too brassy for my tastes. He thinks he has to run the company by the time he's thirty-five or he's not a success." Lloyd began pacing in front of Evelyn's desk, forming some private argument in his own mind.

"Nothing wrong with ambition, Lloyd," Evelyn countered, interrupting his inner dialogue and forcing him to stop in front of her.

He narrowed his gaze on Evelyn and spoke bluntly. "If you had made that comment a few months ago, I would think you believed it. But I've seen the change in you over the last few months. You don't any more approve of Bridgestone's tactics than I do."

Lloyd nodded his head in small victory when Evelyn didn't comment, then turned and left her office, walking to the elevator that would take him up to the office where his pride and joy was waiting for him.

Evelyn dropped the mangled cigarette into the trash, picked up a pencil, then immediately threw it back down onto the desk. Maybe Lloyd was right. She didn't believe all of the old rules. She wasn't so sure of things anymore. But this was still her life, damn it, and she couldn't let all the years of hard work drift away without leaving some reward. She would just have to work harder, accomplish more, press on toward those goals to which she had always aspired.

Glancing at her watch, she realized it was almost time for her luncheon appointment. She was meeting a representative from a large geophysical company at a restaurant halfway across the city. Calculating the time in her head, she knew it would take at least forty-five minutes to get there by taxi. She immediately stood up and grabbed her winter garb from the coat rack, pushed her arms into her tan camel wool coat, donned gloves and scarf, and descended the building in the elevator to brave the bleak, frigid day.

Evelyn looked at her watch for the fourth time in ten minutes and pushed aside the temptation to take more aspirin for her headache. Four o'clock and she still had a huge pile of paperwork on her desk. She had planned to have it all done by the end of the day, but her luncheon meeting had taken longer than she'd expected.

She'd barely made it there on schedule, and by the time they had finished lunch and she'd taken a taxi back to the office, it was after three o'clock.

She shuffled a few papers absently, wondering where on earth to begin. Not able to think clearly enough to even start on it, she once again turned her chair around and stared out of the window.

It had started snowing again about an hour ago, but the flakes were now more like rain, adding to the mushy consistency already on the ground.

Evelyn closed her eyes briefly, wondering what it would be like to see fat, whirling flakes of snow blanketing the mountain peaks of Utah, the sculptured ground downy and trackless except for the occasional deer or bobcat. To hear the breathless silence as it rang eloquently through the canyons. Would the creeks too be covered with snow and ice, while frigid water flowed through tunnels of snow? What would the pine and spruce trees look like draped in heavy clumps of white? Would Michael be lounging on a thickly cushioned couch in front of a crackling fire somewhere, sipping from a mug of hot, spiced wine, his skis propped casually by the door?

Evelyn shook her head violently to dispel the wayward thoughts. No! She had to stop thinking about him. She had sworn to herself that she would never think of him again. Yet, here it was November and she still couldn't purge his image from her mind. He had blended so perfectly with his environment, so strong, so rugged, so untamable. Every time she thought of his touch, hot-cold flashes of excitement swept like fire through her body. He had made her feel more complete than she ever had before in her life. And yet...

He had lied to her. He had used her dependence on him, her need for him, her desire for him, and he had twisted it to serve his own purposes, endangering her life and making her, no doubt, the laughingstock of the entire camp. He was the only man she'd ever cared about and he had destroyed that ability inside her to ever care that much again.

She turned her chair back around with a sigh and finally forced herself to get some work done. She made several phone calls and dictated some letters, all of which pulled her mind back into the folds with which it was most familiar—work.

"Hello, Evelyn." For a moment, the voice did not register and she continued to read a letter in front of her without looking up.

"Still charging through life, I see." Evelyn jumped as the words and the texture of that voice reached her conscious mind. She stared in disbelief at the figure lounging casually against the door frame of her office, his arms crossed in front of him. She continued to stare incredulously at the doorway, not believing that the voice and the figure were anything more than a wandering fancy of her imagination. Suddenly, the image stepped into her office.

She grasped the arms of her chair, holding fast to something concrete and sane. Her breath was lodged in her throat and her gaze was stuck stupidly on his face.

He began to walk slowly around the room, shedding his coat and dropping it on a chair on the opposite side of the desk from where Evelyn sat in near panic. Her fingers were digging into the arms of her chair, her body stiff and tense with fearful anticipation. What was he doing here in New York? In her office? She had never believed she would actually see him again. He was a part of her past, a past she had tried, unsuccessfully, for six months to forget.

With apparent ease, Michael wandered around the room, surveying every detail of the office, the large photographs that depicted nature in all its untouched splendor and in its center an oil derrick. He couldn't help but smirk at the improbability of such an arrangement. He moved on to look at the voluminous rows of reference books on the shelves, the four-drawer file cabinet in the corner, the large U.S. Geological Survey map that dominated one wall.

But all of this was in the periphery of his mind, while his dominant conscious thoughts were on Evelyn sitting so tense and quiet behind her desk. Inside his body, he was one solid ball of nerves. He had thought of this moment for so long, wondered what he would say, how she would react, what the outcome would be. He glanced surreptitiously at her stiff profile and swallowed the impulse to run. Dressed in a gray tailored suit with a mauve silk blouse as the only feminine touch, her hair pulled back into a bun, she appeared totally unapproachable.

The last six months had been a living hell for him. He had wanted so many times to call her, to fly out here to see her. But he had been afraid. Big, brave Michael Baylor had been a coward. He wanted to bide his time and let her harsh memories soften and fade somewhat around the edges. He knew he had hurt her badly, and he wanted some of those wounds to heal a bit before he approached her.

He had never wanted to trick her. But, at the time, it seemed the only way. It was his job to make people test their abilities, to push his students to the limits. But he now knew that he had pushed Evelyn too fast, too far. After she'd left Utah, he reluctantly admitted his true feelings for her. But too late he realized what he'd done to destroy that force between them before it even had a chance to grow and develop.

He had worked the words around in his head so many times since she left, practicing just how he would apologize, exactly what he would say. But now that he was here, the words flew helter-skelter about his mind, all arguments and rationalizations lost in the tense air between them.

All the while Michael calmly moved about, Evelyn's brain was running wildly through the twisted maze of possibilities. What was he doing here? What would she say to him? How could she get rid of him?

She couldn't even trust her voice to speak. Just the sight of him set her blood on fire with a mixture of pain and desire and ire. If he thought he could just walk into her life as if he had done nothing wrong, he had another think coming.

She glared at his back as he looked closely at a photograph on the wall. His shoulders were so broad beneath the gray sweater he had on. He was wearing corduroy jeans over his long, strong legs, and Evelyn's eyes traveled the length of his body with involuntary longing. Gripping the chair harder, she tried to force her thoughts away from the physical draw this man had over her. She hated him! She wanted him to go away!

"What are you doing here? What do you want?" she finally managed to ask, though her voice was an anxious octave too high. He turned away from her books and strolled with seeming casualness back over to the desk, easing himself into a soft leather chair. He folded his hands in his lap, crossed one ankle over the other knee, and watched her with a look that she read as detached interest.

"Still ravishing defenseless women in the wilderness?" she snapped, angry with him for his apparent calm and at herself for her very lack of it.

"Defenseless!" he scoffed, perturbed at himself for letting her get under his skin so quickly. "I certainly hope you're not including yourself in that category. You're about as defenseless as a barracuda."

"Even a barracuda isn't safe around a predaceous shark," she retorted in a voice laden with sarcasm.

Michael stood and leaned toward Evelyn, resting his palms on the desk in front of her. He was so close, he realized; close enough to reach out and touch her if he wanted. If he wanted! That was all he had thought about for the last six months, touching her, holding her beneath him in the grass. And here he was standing over her now, feeling as uncertain as a young boy. "Are you feeling unsafe, Evelyn?" He tried to counteract his own nervousness with arrogance, but his voice came out as a husky whisper. "Is that what it is...? I make you nervous?"

Evelyn's gaze was hypnotically drawn to Michael's mouth, so near, so sensual, so... She shook her head to shake off the spell. "What are you doing here, Michael?" she sighed, turning her chair a little to the left in order to remove the disturbing image of his face from her view. "Are you looking for more executives to enrich? New recruits for your wilderness fun? Well, if that's what you're here for, you're wasting your time with me. I'm a wounded veteran of that war, remember, and I have no intention whatsoever of re-enlisting."

Michael sat wearily back down in the chair. "I'm here on business, but not for the school, Evelyn."

She looked dubious. What other kind of business could he possibly be here for? "What kind of business?" she asked bluntly.

"The headquarters of the company I work for is here in New York."

"Expanding Horizons is headquartered here?" she asked with skepticism.

"No." He watched the confusion flicker across her face, and realized she hadn't even listened to him that day in Utah. "I told you I was a lawyer, Evelyn."

"A...lawyer! You never told—" She stopped, remembering the day in the wilderness when he had accused her of being a snob. He'd asked her if she would feel better if he said he was a lawyer, but she hadn't realized that he was serious. "I thought...you were joking. You're not a—you're a lawyer?"

"Yes."

"With a New York law firm?" she asked incredulously.

"No," he explained, "I'm a corporate lawyer with Impex."

"The mining company?"

He nodded and her mind began to reel with this new bit of information about him. She thought she knew exactly who and what Michael Baylor was. She thought that all he did was teach in that wilderness school. She had no idea that that was only a part-time endeavor. "How do you have the time to teach at Expanding Horizons?"

"I make time," he stated simply. "It's very important to me."

Evelyn cast her eyes away from his direct gaze, cringing inside as she thought of that night in New York so long ago when she'd spoken to him as if he were nothing more than a provincial cowhand who spent his after-hours hanging around the local tavern, guzzling pitchers of beer with the boys.

"Well, I see," she said after a long while.

"What do you see, Evelyn?" Michael had leaned forward in his chair, his elbows on his knees and his hands clasped in front of him, and his voice had a seeking quality to it, as if he were appealing to her for something that was beyond both of their minds.

Flustered both by his tone of voice and by the question, Evelyn spoke through tightly held lips. "I see I've made an ass of myself."

Michael looked startled for a brief moment, then perplexed. "Evelyn...you didn't...I'm the one who acted like a fool."

They looked at each other then, quizzical expressions revealing that neither one had ever understood the thoughts or motives of the other.

"There you are, Michael." Lloyd broke the moment between them by poking his head in through the doorway of her office. "I should have known this is where I'd find you," he smiled all-knowingly, causing Evelyn to frown in bewilderment.

How would Lloyd have known that? And why was he looking for Michael in the first place?

Michael turned around and smiled at Lloyd but wished silently that he could have had a few more minutes alone with Evelyn. He had so much to say to her, and so far none of it had come out of his mouth.

"Did you persuade this lovely lady to have dinner with us?" Lloyd asked as he patted Michael on the back.

"Well, no," Michael shrugged. "We didn't get quite that far."

Evelyn frowned again at Lloyd. "I thought you were having dinner with your god—" She stopped, something vague and disturbing clutching at her insides. No, it couldn't be. No, that's ridic— She shifted her narrowed gaze to Michael and then back to Lloyd. "Your . . . godson."

She leaned her forearms on the desk, clasping her hands tightly in front of her, her mind clouding with the overload of information she had received in the last few minutes. Godson! As she glanced back and forth between the two men, vague bits of past conversations and remembrances came to her. They were things that had not really registered when she'd first heard them, but now they crawled up from her subconscious, marching before her with crystal clarity. Lloyd's godson had served in Vietnam. He was a lawyer. His name was Michael. Michael's parents had died when he was seventeen. He had been raised by a friend of the family. And, too, Roger's words—"I guess he's just that extra little bit of added insurance"—when she'd first met Michael suddenly took on a new significance. Added insurance. Her boss's godson!

"You're his . . . He's your . . . ?"

"Didn't you know Michael was my godson, Evelyn?" Lloyd seemed genuinely surprised. After all, he had talked about him so much over the years.

"No," she whispered, anger building in every fiber of her body. When she again spoke to Lloyd, her words were drawn out painfully, rising louder with each syllable. "This is the same damned...damned...idiot I've been hearing about for God only knows how many years?"

"Evelyn!" Lloyd's face turned livid with righteous indignation. "You have no right to—"

"It's okay, Lloyd," Michael stood up and clasped the man's shoulder affectionately. "She's just surprised, aren't you, Evelyn?" Michael's face had hardened slightly as he turned toward her, a subtle warning adrift in his eyes.

"Surprised? Surprised!" She was now standing, her fingers clutching the edge of her desk. "Surprised is hardly the emotion I am feeling right now. Anger is closer to it, although that too is a bit inadequate. But I certainly understand now. Oh, yes, I get the picture all right. You two clever boys plotted this little thing all along, didn't you?"

"Don't, Evelyn." Michael's jaw clenched tightly in direct warning, but she was past the point of being intimidated by him.

"You two must have had lots of fun planning and scheming for my humiliation, for my—"

"What on earth?" Lloyd was stunned by her accusations and her anger.

"And, Michael, how convenient for you not to tell me this little bit of information in Utah," she snarled sarcastically.

With that, Michael walked swiftly around the desk and grasped her shoulders. "You would have liked that, wouldn't you?" he growled in a low whisper.

"You would have liked having one more reason to use me to get where you want to go, I'll bet. Shall we tell Lloyd about the little contract we made that first night? Should we tell him what considerations you bargain with? No, I didn't tell you about my relationship with Lloyd because I was afraid of what you would do with that information. I did it to protect myself. I wanted to remain innocent about how far you'd go with ammunition like that."

"Excuse me, Miss Scott?" Evelyn's secretary stuck her head around the door, the expression of bewilderment and apology on her face attesting to the fact that she'd heard the thunderous sounds of battle from her desk in the outer office. Michael and Evelyn flinched and drew apart quickly, and Evelyn forced her attention toward the girl. "I'm sorry to—to bother you, but Mr. Evans from GeoSeis is on the line. Do you want to talk?"

"Tell him I'll call him tomorrow, Carolyn," Evelyn said, a sudden surge of weariness drawing all strength from her body.

When the secretary had returned to her post to handle the phone call, Evelyn pulled open a drawer to reach her purse, walked to the coat rack and grabbed her coat, gloves, and hat, then turned back to the two men.

"Lloyd, did you plan this with Michael?" Her eyes were dull with fatigue and shock.

"Evelyn." Lloyd stepped toward her awkwardly. "I don't know what's going on here between the two of you." He glanced back and forth between them for a moment. "But if you mean did Michael and I talk about whether you should go to Utah, the answer is yes. He had apparently met you and thought the program would be good for you. I had mentioned that you were an executive-bound employee and so . . . it was decided that you would go."

She looked at him dubiously, waiting for the next revelation. "And?" she asked snidely.

"You listen to me," Michael exploded, grabbing her arm again in his powerful grip. "What I did to you in Utah had—and has—nothing to do with Lloyd. Don't involve him in this."

Slowly extracting her arm from his grasp, Evelyn sighed heavily. "I really don't want to talk about this anymore." She waved her hand distractedly. "It really doesn't matter anymore. I—I just want to go home." She lethargically slipped her arms into her coat, picked up her purse and walked toward the door of her office. Turning at the last minute toward her boss, she stammered, "I-I'm sorry, Lloyd. I guess I'm just tired, that's all."

She walked out, closing the door behind her and leaving the two men inside her office with their own very private and concerned thoughts about her behavior.

Damn! Michael closed his eyes briefly in self-disgust. He'd blown it. He'd said all the wrong things, let his anger get the best of him, and allowed Evelyn to leave without him even apologizing for what he'd done to her.

"Damn! What am I going to do, Lloyd?" Michael shook his head in frustration and sat down on the corner of the desk.

"You know, Michael, that's the first time you've asked my advice on anything since you got out of the service.'' Despite his confusion, Lloyd's mouth held a secret smile of gratitude. "Let's go get a drink and we'll talk.''

Michael nodded then picked up his coat from the chair, walked over to the man who had been his father since he was seventeen, placed his arm around the older man's shoulder, and together the two men walked out of the office.

Chapter Eight

"How deep do you think that number two well is going to be, Bill?" Tom asked, taking a large gulp of his drink, then signaling the waiter for another. The question unfortunately triggered a whole new round of technical shoptalk. Evelyn rolled her eyes and tried very hard not to yawn in response to the conversation around her. Without a doubt, Tom Bridgestone had to be one of the most boring people in the whole world. And Bill Radden was just about as bad.

Dressed to the hilt in their three-piece pinstriped suits, their fifty-dollar haircuts lending just the right touch of casual elegance to their looks, the two men would have to be described as dashing. And Mary, Bill's date, who looked chic in her silk shirtwaist, her scarf draped with studied casualness around her neck so that the designer label was—coincidentally—in full view, was the height of sophistication.

Evelyn had to be honest and admit to herself that six months ago, she sounded and looked exactly like these three people. And she marveled at how a person's character—how her own personality—could change so much in that short a time.

After leaving the office that afternoon, she had taken a taxi through the slush-covered streets to her apartment building. She couldn't remember ever feeling as exhausted as she was this afternoon. Too many sensations, too much information, and far too many memories had assailed her the moment Michael walked into her office.

His presence before her had conjured up all the longings and needs for him that she had tried so hard to suppress. He had appeared so healthy, so robust compared to the typical New Yorker in winter. His hair was a little shorter than it had been in June, more in keeping with the corporate business that brought him here. And shining from that tanned face were the eyes that had haunted Evelyn for so many months. Cobalt-blue eyes that pierced her to the core, rendering her as incapable of independent thought or action as an insect pinned against a burlap canvas for inspection.

And she had been unable to handle the glut of information that she had received today in her office. Michael was Lloyd's godson, a corporate lawyer! That revelation had seemed so incriminating this afternoon when she first heard it. But after she went home and relaxed her mind and body in the bathtub for a while, letting the tension slowly drain out of her, the revelation had fallen into a perspective that she could handle. Now she could see that Lloyd would not have had anything to do with Michael's behavior. He was not a deceitful kind of person. No, Michael was totally responsible for his own actions. The blame could be placed on no one but himself.

"Evelyn? Evelyn, are you in there?" Tom waved a hand in front of her.

"Oh, yes. I'm sorry. What did you say?" Evelyn was startled out of her ruminations and was forced to recognize the presence of her three co-workers.

"I was wondering if you wanted another drink." Tom smiled solicitously.

"No, I'm fine," she answered with a weak smile, glancing at her still full glass of scotch. The other three were already on their second round of drinks. Bad start to the evening, Evelyn reprimanded herself. Rule number one: You'll only isolate yourself from your business associates if you don't keep up with their drinking.

Evelyn had decided that Tom and Mary and Bill would all be considered hard-chargers in Michael's book. The whiz kids of the eighties, their lives were geared toward nothing but success. All they could ever talk about was work, because that was their only interest. They were the types of employees who spent every Saturday in the office, only in part to catch up on work but primarily to be seen by their superiors. Or if they indulged in pastime activities such as tennis or racketball, it was always pursued as a work-related skill.

That convoluted web was such a vicious one in which to be caught and only six short months ago Evelyn too had been snared by it. The difference now was that she could see that it was a trap, that it was a substitute for a more meaningful life. Now she accepted the truth that she had followed the path she did because she knew how to do nothing else. And yet she couldn't break the ties that bound her to that ever-turning wheel. Here she was out to dinner with people she thought of as raving bores. What was it she needed?

What did she want out of life? And why could she no longer force these impertinent, probing questions to the back of her mind?

"Did you know that lodge-pole pines are usually the first trees to sprout after a forest fire?" Evelyn smiled sweetly at the three blank faces that stared back at her.

After a tangible pause, Mary cleared her throat in embarrassment and turned to face Tom. "Did Bob Muldoon call you the other day about that property in Oklahoma?"

"Yes." As an expression of relief washed across his face Tom leaned into the table with excitement. "In fact, he told me that..."

As the conversation resumed its normal, narrow course, Evelyn smiled inwardly and went back to playing with her silverware. She sipped lightly on her drink and turned around to watch the dinner crowd flowing into Carmello's. The maitre d' checked his reservations list, then after a short wait the patrons were led to one of the linen-draped tables.

"What's happening in Bolivia, Evelyn? Did Antron get the bid?" All eyes riveted on Evelyn and she was again forced to participate in their discussion.

"We're hoping it will go through," she replied non-committally. The project was still in the negotiation stage and the less said about it, the better. Still, it would be an important acquisition for Antron, and questions about its possibilities were inevitable. "We should know something more definite in another week or two. Frank Groden is doing most of the negotiating with the Bolivian government, so we'll just have to wait and see."

"Frank's a good man for the job," Bill said, and Evelyn had to agree despite her personal animosities toward the man.

"I just hope the political situation remains stable until the job is completed," Mary inserted, and each of them agreed that that was a prime consideration in the deal.

Evelyn didn't want to have to divulge anything of importance, so she was relieved when the waiter finally brought the menus. She began perusing the list of scrumptious entrees when she heard Tom chuckle derisively and say, "Take a look at that character over there. He looks like he belongs on a sheep ranch."

"Can you believe anyone would come to Carmello's in jeans and a sheepskin coat?" Mary's face reflected the astonishment in her voice.

Evelyn's back was to the door, so she couldn't see the object of her companions' scorn, yet her heart began pounding so loudly she was sure everyone at the table would hear it. She only knew one man who would so blatantly buck the system by appearing at an elegant restaurant dressed that way. That man could care less about propriety and, in fact, probably cultivated his offbeat image.

Evelyn's hands were clamped together in her lap, her fingers squeezing tightly to hold in the trembling emotions that were rolling through her. Before she could form a clear definition as to what those emotions were, he was standing beside her chair and she was looking up into Michael Baylor's cobalt-blue eyes.

Michael looked down at Evelyn. She was wearing a soft, yellow silk dress that tied at the waist, the color a perfect contrast for her blue eyes. Her long black hair was swept back on one side and held with a thin, gold barrette. He looked at her hands clasped tightly in her lap, her knuckles white with the strain. What was she feeling? Fear? Anger? There was something so vulnerable about her tension that he wanted to run his hand down the back of her hair, across her shoulder and down her back, easing the tautness from her body.

"Hi," he said softly, speaking only to her as if the others were not sitting there.

Evelyn's eyes were fastened on Michael's face, watching him as he watched her. His eyes were like fingers touching her, sliding down her back and across her flesh. She forcefully shook the thrill of pleasure from her mind and body and straightened her back to ward off his invading presence.

"Hello," she replied tightly, afraid to soften any part of her toward him. Though he was, indeed, wearing his sheep-lined coat, every fiber in Evelyn's body was aware of the masculinity in his presence. Every man in the crowded restaurant paled in comparison to Michael. But she intensified her efforts to appear unconcerned by his presence here and began blandly introducing him to her co-workers.

"Tom, Mary, Bill, this is Michael Baylor," she recited in a monotone that belied her tumultuous emotions. "He is an attor—" She stopped, staring down at the design on her plate. How was she to introduce him to these people? How she saw him was nothing like they would see him. To her, he was not an attorney; he was her instructor at the wilderness school, her nemesis, her lover, her enemy, the man of her fantasies and nightmares—the man she was most determined to vanquish from her mind. "He's from Utah," she finally said, and missed the slightly amused twist of Michael's mouth. "Michael, this is Tom, Mary, and Bill. Friends of mine from the office."

The men extended hands and shook. "It's a pleasure to meet you." Mary tilted her head a little to the right, trying to decide if she should laugh at his outfit or throw herself at his incredible body.

"Won't you join us for dinner?" Tom asked with a sideways flicker of sadistic delight cast toward Mary and Bill. Evelyn watched the exchange and felt a momentary flash of anger at the three of them. She didn't want him sitting here beside her, looking at her. She didn't want to have to listen to his voice. Besides, she knew what mischief they were up to. They were only inviting him to sit down because they wanted to see how entertaining this yokel from Utah could be.

"I thought you were eating with ... someone else tonight." She caught herself at the last moment before saying Lloyd's name. All these three needed was to hear that and they would be fawning over Michael all night to get in Lloyd's good graces.

"There was a change of plans," he smiled, knowing exactly why she was purposefully vague in her question.

"Oh." She turned her face away, her mouth drawing downward. Michael removed his coat, then seated himself at the round table in the chair to the right of Evelyn.

"So, Michael, are you a cowboy?" Evelyn grimaced as she heard Tom's idiotic question, knowing it was the same close-minded impression she had had of him when she first met him last February.

"Michael is a wilderness instructor," Evelyn related blandly, wishing now that the conversation would switch back to something emotionally safe like oil exploration.

"Really," Tom drawled boredly. "Where? At that school you went to, Evelyn?"

"Yes." She stared at the centerpiece, avoiding eye contact with anyone at the table.

"The name is Expanding Horizons," Michael smiled.

"Really," Evelyn's date intoned again. "And what is one supposed to expand at this school?" he asked with a superior tilt of his head.

"Oh, lots of things," Michael answered. "Sometimes even one's vocabulary."

Tom's face hardened at the derogatory remark. "Really," he slurred slowly and with malice.

Michael smiled his friendliest smile. "Really."

"I can't imagine having to go through all that." Mary shivered dramatically. "I understand it's pretty rough."

"Tell us," Bill laughed, leaning conspiratorially toward Michael. "How did Evelyn do? Did you have to carry her the whole way?"

Tom and Mary joined in the laughter, and Evelyn felt the heat from Michael's hot, penetrating stare on the side of her face.

"Are we not going to eat tonight?" she snapped, looking across the restaurant to signal the waiter. "I'm dying to try the prime rib." She caught the waiter's attention and was relieved that he immediately came to the table, giving her an excuse to change the subject.

They each gave their order to the waiter, Tom and Mary ordering escargot, Bill deciding on lobster, and Michael ordering the largest filet on the menu.

"We want wine, don't we?" Bill asked.

"Why don't we let Mr. Baylor order the wine for

us," Tom suggested in a voice that left no doubt as to his dislike of Michael.

Michael nodded and the waiter handed him the wine list, waiting patiently for his decision. Evelyn twisted her napkin nervously in her lap, furious with her colleagues for playing such sadistic games and angry at herself for even caring whether Michael made a fool of himself or not. Why should she care? After all he had humiliated her in front of the entire wilderness camp.

"They will have the Château Montrachet," Michael informed the waiter, then smiled at Tom's disconcerted expression, causing an unconscious sparkle in Evelyn's eyes.

"Very good selection, sir," the waiter bowed slightly. "Will there be anything else?"

"Yes, I'll have a beer."

The waiter cleared his throat. "Lowenbrau, sir?"

"Olympia, if you have it." Michael grinned at the waiter's disgusted, but still servile countenance.

"Very . . . good, sir," he responded tightly, then walked away, shaking his head in bemusement.

To hide his own irritation at Michael's ability in selecting the wine, and ignoring the subtle ridicule of the group that was evident when Michael ordered his beer, Tom turned his attention to Bill and Mary, explaining a new drilling device he had seen at the Oil Technology Conference the month before.

Evelyn finally looked up at Michael in reprimand. "You delight in doing things like that, don't you?" she whispered, trying not to show her amusement over the scene.

"Well, honestly, Evelyn," he whispered back, "where on earth did you dig up these flatheads?"

She giggled despite herself and Tom, perhaps realizing that she was laughing at them, shot her a look of indignation.

When the food arrived, conversation was kept light and inconsequential. Michael fielded questions about the school from Bill and Mary and even occasionally from Tom. Tom had mellowed somewhat from his earlier hostility and Evelyn, refusing to admit that it had anything to do with Michael's easy charm, attributed the friendlier attitude to the wine.

When the conversation once again returned to work-related events, Michael rose from his chair and grasped Evelyn's elbow. "Let's go dance."

Evelyn stared up at his imposing figure, hearing for the first time the strains of soft music flowing from the bar. The dim lighting in the restaurant had softened the blue of Michael's eyes, but they still held the same intimate persuasion that filtered like heady wine into her bloodstream. His fingers on her elbow were like red-hot irons chaining her to him, body and soul.

She parted her lips to say no, but no sound was uttered. Instead she was effortlessly lifted to her feet and led, slowly winding through the tables, toward the soft love songs being played by the dance band.

What was she doing this for? Evelyn cried inwardly as Michael wrapped his right arm around her waist and pulled her into the rhythm of his steps. She hated him for what he had done to her in Utah! She didn't want him coming back into her life upsetting her equilibrium again. Whenever she was in his arms, she felt as if she were falling and there was nothing to hold her back, nothing to support her except for him. If he let go again, as he did in Utah when he left her alone in the wilderness, she might never regain her balance. She didn't need him in her life. She had to get him out!

She tried to pull away from him before it was too late, but he held her fast.

"You thought all I knew how to do was the Cotton-Eyed Joe, didn't you?" he whispered huskily against her neck.

"What?" she stammered, not having the faintest idea who this cotton-eye Joe person was, knowing only that she wanted desperately to make her escape before her soul was taken prisoner again.

He chuckled lightly and pulled her close. "Relax, Evelyn. The workday is over and you need—"

"Workday!" she whispered venomously. "Is that why you think I'm wanting to get away from you? Because I want to sit with those idiots and talk about work!"

Michael pulled his head back and looked down at her, his pulse accelerating at the closeness of her mouth to his own. "Then what?" he asked softly, almost afraid to hear the truth come from her mouth.

"If you think I have forgotten what happened in Utah—what you did to me—then you are sadly mistaken. I haven't forgotten it and I never will," she added with force.

"Nor will I, Evelyn. I haven't forgotten one thing that happened between us. Not one touch, one—"

"I'm not talking about that, Michael, and you know it," she whispered with a trembling voice, angry with herself for the weakness that flooded through her limbs at the thought of those shared moments of love. "I'm talking about the way you tricked me, humiliated me, placed me in danger when you knew I was not prepared for something like that.''

Michael's mouth was tightly drawn and his eyes were watching her carefully, almost nervously she decided.

"I trusted you, Michael, and you purposely destroyed that trust." Evelyn's voice was shaking badly, revealing the gaping wound that resisted all of her attempts to cauterize it. "I will never forgive you for that!"

They were standing still now, no longer moving their bodies with the music. His arm was still around her, his left hand clasping her right, but they did not move. She was staring blankly at his chest, unseeing, unmoving, waiting to hear whatever excuses he had for his behavior. It took several moments to realize that what he uttered was not an excuse at all.

"What did you say?" She finally looked up at him.

"I said, I don't blame you. I did an unforgivable thing." His expression was grim as he gazed down at her. "I made a mistake, a terrible one."

Evelyn realized he had loosened his hold on her body and she was free to go. She stood still, watching him with anxious eyes. Why hadn't he tried to exonerate himself with some worthless excuse—one that she could ridicule and then turn and walk away? By making no excuses, by blaming himself entirely, he had left her defenses against him weaker than ever. He was too vulnerable like this, making his hold over her even more powerful than before. Now what was she going to do about him?

The band began a new piece, soft and seductive, and she found herself enclosed once again in Michael's arms. But this time, he wrapped both arms around her waist, making her fit perfectly into the contours of his body. Her cheek was leaning against his chest, the top of her head tucked beneath his chin.

"I've missed you, Evelyn." His voice rushed like a soft breeze through her hair. "Come with me to my apartment. Spend the night with me."

Her eyes fell closed as his words melted into her flesh and she wanted nothing more at that moment than to go home with him and lie in his arms for the rest of the night. But she could not.

She didn't trust him. Too much had happened, their lives and their philosophies too different. She belonged back at the table with Tom and Bill and Mary, discussing the things that would push her farther into a future that left no room for abstract thoughts, for unanswerable doubts, for untamed explorations into the spirit. Success in the business world was the core of her life. It was the one thing that would provide her with the assurance of always being needed. It was her security blanket and buffer against a world that to her was cold and unfeeling, a world that had been unkind since she was thirteen years old.

She pulled from his embrace. "No, Michael. I'm going back to the table now." She turned to head back into the restaurant.

"Evelyn." He clasped his large hand around her wrist. He opened his mouth with words that might change her mind, but she did not give him the chance to speak.

"No, Michael," she spoke softly but forcefully. "No."

He watched her as she walked away from him, passing through the doorway of the bar into the restaurant,

her back straight and her head held high and determined.

As she fitfully tossed and turned to the right the digital
clock on the bedside table glowed back at her with the
time. One-thirty and she still wasn't asleep. She had
been pitching and squirming from one side of the bed
to the other, punching her pillow, and realigning her
covers for the last hour and a half. Still, sleep would not
come.

She had come back home at ten-thirty, declining
Tom's invitation to join the three of them at his apartment for drinks. Instead, she had wanted nothing more
than to come home and sleep off the drugging effect
that Michael had induced in her.

After she'd left him on the dance floor, he'd returned to the table only to pick up his coat, and after a
polite and cool good-bye, he left the restaurant. She
tried to ignore the snide remarks that Tom made about
Michael behind his back and had found the topics of
conversation around her even more tedious and dull
than ever.

It had been a relief when she finally returned to the
sanctity of her own apartment, where she could forget
the entire painful evening.

Flinging the covers back with her legs, Evelyn now
realized how ridiculous that delusion had been. She
could not forget one thing about this evening. Neither
the touch of Michael's hand against her lower back, nor
the way the breath of his voice fell across the top of her
head as they danced. Nor could she forget the sensations in her own body when she was dancing so close to
him.

She pushed herself from the bed. Damn! Michael invaded every square inch of her life. When was she going to be able to forget him? They had had an affair, a brief interlude. But she had to forget it and get on with her life the way she had planned it.

She walked over to the chaise longue next to the window and stretched her body out on it. Flicking the curtain aside with her hand, she watched the moon trying to peek out from behind the gray clouds. No stars were visible tonight and she couldn't help but compare this night sky with that of those nights in Utah where it was so clear she could see forever, looking back into time at light that was propelled from its source long before the earth was even inhabited with human beings.

The cold, gray, limited sky of New York seemed a perfect metaphor for the narrow existence in which Evelyn lived. Her vision was directed down only the narrow tunnel of her professional life, never looking beyond at other possibilities and options that might be open to her.

Watching in an exhausted daze for the occasional glimpses of the stars and moon, she soon fell asleep. But her mind was not blessed with the respite it so badly needed. She dreamt that she was curled up inside a too-tight sleeping bag, and her feet and face were ice cold while the rest of her body sweltered beneath the down quilting. Without warning, she began rolling down a hill, still wrapped tightly in the sleeping bag, bouncing and crashing over rocks and tree stumps as she continued to tumble down the mountainside. Before she reached bottom, her nightmare abruptly switched scenes and she was standing on the Flea's Leap, Michael on the rock below her with his arms outstretched, waiting for her to jump to him. Though his mouth did not move, the words "Trust me" flowed from between his smiling lips, bouncing in echoes off the canyon walls. Squeezing her eyes closed tightly, Evelyn jumped toward Michael's waiting arms but, at the last minute, he moved to the side letting her fall down into the abyss, the canyon floor thousands of feet down the only barrier that would eventually stop her fall.

When her body hit the floor with a thud beside the chaise longue, Evelyn's eyes opened wide in fright and confusion. She was trembling with an impotent kind of rage that soon broke into tears of despair coursing down her cheeks and onto the front of her nightgown.

"Damn you, Michael Baylor!" she whispered into the dark. "I don't need you, and I don't trust you!"

She looked up at the now clear night sky that had finally pushed away the clouds, and groaned. *And I hate you for making me lie even to myself.*

Chapter Nine

A loud rapping at the door of her apartment began to intersect her brain waves, causing a vague disturbance in her sleep, but she ignored it. It would surely go away and let her enjoy what little rest she had as yet received. The banging on the door sounded again, louder and more insistent this time.

"All right, all right," Evelyn mumbled grouchily, dragging herself and half the covers off the bed. Stumbling to the closet, more by sense than by sight, she rummaged around in the closet until she found her blue velour caftan. She slipped into it and resumed feeling her way to the door. "Who is it?" she yawned and leaned against the wall with her eyes closed.

"Rise and shine, princess."

Her eyes immediately flew open, all sleep receding into a night that was now past tense. Oh, no! She grasped the robe around her throat in an involuntary reflex to the sound of that unwanted presence. What was he doing here at this hour? What on earth did he want with her now?

Michael frowned at the silence that greeted him from the other side of the door. Maybe she wasn't going to

open it and let him in. But she had to! He had so many
things to talk to her about, things that hadn't been said
last night. He hadn't really considered the possibility
that she might not let him in. That didn't fit the game
plan at all. He tried to force his positive thoughts to
coincide with her conscious mind, willing her hand to
reach out and turn the doorknob.

"Go away," came the anxious reply instead.

He grimaced. Well, so much for mental telepathy.
"Come on, Evelyn, please. I need to talk to you."

"You and I have nothing to say to one another. And
how did you get past the doorman anyway?" she
snipped.

"I lied to him," he answered without a trace of re-
morse.

"That doesn't surprise me," she muttered, leaning
weakly with her back against the door. The sound of his
voice alone was enough to turn the bones in her body
to jelly, and though she didn't want him to come inside, she realized with fatalistic truth that she did not
have the strength to keep him out.

Michael listened to the clicking, sliding sounds of
dead bolts and chain locks being unfastened. Evelyn
flung open the door in exasperation directed both at
herself and at Michael. She was struck at once by his
vibrant, robust appearance. He was dressed in a navy-
blue jogging suit and Adidas running shoes. In his hand
was a green ski hat with the name Snowbird spelled out
in red letters. After her eyes had traveled unconsciously along the length of his body and then returned to his
face, she blushed at the hint of a victorious smile that
touched his mouth.

Michael stepped into the room and watched silently
as Evelyn closed the door, but his brows were knitted

as she relatched what seemed to him an excessive number of locks, even for New York City.

"What do you want, Michael?" Evelyn asked, self-consciously fingering the folds of her robe as he scanned her apartment.

The entryway opened into a spacious living room of soft pastels and sectional furniture. The graphics on the walls looked expensive and in perfect harmony with the decor. Not exactly his cup of tea, Michael noted. But still, one had to appreciate the work and expense that must have gone into creating this sumptuous environment.

He looked back at her and gazed with awe at the outline of her body beneath the robe. "That's what you had on that night you came to the lodge porch," he breathed huskily in wonderment, taking a step toward her.

She stepped back to avoid the onslaught of an explosive invasion for which she had no defense. There was no armor in her arsenal to ward off this type of an attack from him. She had found out before how futile her attempts at that were. The bone structure in her limbs began to weaken as he continued to gaze at her with open desire.

"Michael, did you come here to torment me?" she asked in a tremulous voice.

Hearing that frightened tone in her voice, he glanced up, silent and thoughtful. "No, Evelyn," he finally answered in a deep voice. "I don't want to torment you." He couldn't begin to tell her what he really wanted. He couldn't even form the words.

He glanced at his own attire. "Actually, I came by to go jogging with you."

"Jogging!"

"Sure," he smiled, trying to ease the tension between them. "Lloyd told me you started jogging after you came back from Utah."

"Well, yes," she groaned, "but not in sub-zero weather."

"It's a gorgeous day out there, Evelyn." Michael's face was lit with that infectious ingredient she knew so well. "The sun is shining and—"

"It's ten degrees, right?"

"No," he hedged. "Twenty-five."

"Forget it," she said, then turned in dismissal to go to the kitchen and fix a pot of coffee.

"I see. In other words, Lloyd exaggerated when he said you jog." Michael remained standing in the same spot and baited her with his voice. "Well, I figured it was too good to be true. I guess you lady executives are busy enough trying to keep up mentally with the business world. I suppose it would be too much to expect you to find the time for anything physical."

She pivoted sharply and pressed a hand on her side, her eyes narrowing ominously. "I jog."

"Sure." His smile was patronizing and skeptical.

Evelyn whirled away from the kitchen and stalked into the bedroom where she slammed the door.

Michael smiled again, this time in sure victory, as he sauntered over to the plush, peach-colored couch and sat down, flipping through a *Fortune* magazine that lay on the glass-topped coffee table.

Within minutes, the door to the bedroom swung back open, and Evelyn, dressed in a soft plum jogging outfit, replete with matching running shoes and sweat band, strode purposefully toward the front door of her apartment. Unlatching the locks, she turned with a superior air toward Michael. "Are you coming or not?" she snapped impatiently, tapping her foot against the floor of the marble entryway.

Michael chuckled and tossed the magazine back onto the table. "After you." He quirked an eyebrow upward and extended his hand toward the door.

When the first blast of cold air hit Evelyn's lungs, she felt as if they would explode from the force. She'd tried to psych herself up for this all the way down in the elevator, but nothing could have prepared her for the icy pain that now gripped her chest. True, she had been jogging the last few months, but never in weather like this. Her exercise had been reserved primarily for gentle fall days, when the air first began to lose its flush, adding instead a crisp bite that was refreshing but never cold.

This—well this was plain suicide. And all she wanted to do was crawl back into bed under her nice warm blankets. But there was no way she was going to let Michael know how she felt. No way was she going to let him think that she couldn't handle this. She would show him that she could not only keep up, but possibly even surpass him.

Against her better judgment, Evelyn began running full out as soon as they reached the park, and Michael merely shook his head behind her in bemusement. He took a few easy strides and caught up with her, chuckling inwardly at her stubborn determination.

"Lovely day, isn't it?" he grinned, jogging along at an even pace with her, ducking under a thick tree branch that arched across the pathway.

"Lovely," she quipped, sounding much brighter and more chipper than she felt.

Michael turned his attention to the skyscape rising from behind the trees. "You know, every time I come back to this city I'm amazed at how much different it looks from the way I remembered it. I lived here for several years and yet I seem to forget so many things about it when I'm away. Have you ever lived anywhere else?"

"No," she answered breathlessly, her legs aching already from the pounding of her heels against the pavement.

"I didn't think so."

"And just what, may I ask, is that supposed to mean?" Evelyn glared pointedly at him before turning her attention back to the path upon which she was running.

Michael returned the pointed stare and shrugged. "It means you have that... city look. It's an air about you, a quality."

"I'm sure you mean that as an insult," she sneered, never slowing her pace, but aware of the strain on her body every time she tried to talk.

Michael was silent for a long moment before speaking. "I didn't say that."

"I suppose you'd prefer women who are more like Dorothy Miller," Evelyn said, hating herself for the jealous tone that crept into her voice.

Michael tried hard not to smile. "Well, that all depends. Now, if I wanted someone to help me build a log cabin or fell a few trees, then sure, I'd definitely pick someone like Dorothy. On the other hand"—he smiled crookedly—"if my cabin were already built and I was wanting someone to warm my bed..."

At a fork in the pathway, Evelyn turned sharply to

the right, hoping to lose Michael. It turned out to be a poor attempt at best.

Michael caught up with her easily and grasped her elbow to slow her down. 'Evelyn, did you know I was with you the whole time you thought you were alone in the mountains?''

Evelyn's feet slowed and her breathing completely stopped for a few agonizing seconds. She stared at the cold, hard ground in front of her, not daring to look at Michael's face. After only a few moments' pause, she once again picked up her pace, trying to run fast in order to leave that topic of conversation behind.

Michael had no trouble catching up with her. "Did you know that, Evelyn?" He wasn't going to let the subject drop. They had to talk about this, get beyond it, before their relationship could go anywhere. "I never let you out of my sight for one minute."

Evelyn stopped and bent forward, her hands on her thighs and her breath discharging in ragged gasps. She wanted to keep running, to get away from Michael and his explanations and rationalizations of what he did to her, but she could not. Her legs and her lungs would go no farther. She felt his hand on her arm, pulling her up straight and she had no energy left to fight him.

"I would never have left you alone in the mountains, Evelyn," he spoke softly and his eyes, like molten minerals, pleaded with her to believe him. His hand was still grasping her arm and his fingers tightened with the intensity of his feelings.

"I know that I never should have made the bargain in the first place. It was idiotic. There was no way in hell I could carry it through, and I knew that. But I also knew that I had to make love to you." His eyes shifted restlessly along the ground before lifting to her face. "I let the fact that I wanted you override my better judgment."

"That's why you left me in the wilderness," she retorted sarcastically.

"Evelyn, I had to show you what you could do for yourself."

"All right, you showed me," she responded tightly. "Now it's over. It's in the past so I really don't think we need to talk about it anymore."

"It's not over. And it won't be until we come to an understanding about it. We have to get beyond this, Evelyn, or our relationship is at a standstill."

"Our relationship, Michael!" she gasped for air. "Our relationship, if there ever was one of any significance, ended six months ago. It is at a standstill because it has nowhere to go. It is dead! A casualty of the war."

"You're wrong, Evelyn, and you know it as well as I do. Last night when we were dancing was the first time I was sure of it."

"Sure of what?" she asked in exasperation.

"Sure of your feelings for me. We have something special, Evelyn. You know it and I know it. I just turned thirty-nine and I've never had feelings for another woman like the ones I have for you."

"Well, I'd say that's your problem and not mine." She pulled her arm free and began walking back in the direction of her apartment building.

He hesitated, watching her until she was about twenty yards ahead of him. In a sudden burst of renewed confidence, he jogged up behind her and clasped onto her upper arm, holding her beside him as they walked. "I've spent a lot of restless years, Evelyn, and this is only the second time I've felt totally sure about something. The first time," he explained when he caught her quick sideways glance, "was when I decided to move back to the mountains."

Evelyn was still walking, but he could tell she was listening at the same time, so he continued.

"When I decided I'd had enough drifting, I came home to live with Lloyd and Margaret, and enrolled in law school. I was twenty-nine when I graduated and got my first job. Can you believe that—twenty-nine!"

"You were in the service. That was a job,". Evelyn responded in a tight voice, finding herself drawn inescapably into the conversation. "And you were a ski instructor."

Michael shook his head. "Nope. Neither of those count. I knew I owed it to my father and to Lloyd to try and accomplish something worthwhile. And teaching spoiled little rich girls how to snowplow is hardly what I would call worthwhile." He laughed.

"Yes, but what about ... ?"

Michael glanced at Evelyn sharply, raising his hand to keep the words from being uttered. "Don't even say it," he spoke slowly and precisely, holding in whatever frustration remained from those eighteen months overseas. "Taking a hill one day and then giving it back the next..." He was silent for several long moments before continuing. "Anyway," he breathed deeply. "I needed to do something constructive with my life, so I got a job in the legal department of Impex. Knowing that they had offices all over the West, I secretly hoped that I would be given a transfer to Utah or Colorado before long."

Evelyn had slowed her pace and was listening with rapt attention as Michael's past unfolded before her.

"But it's funny," he was saying. "I got caught up in this obsessive drive for success. I lived, breathed, ate, drank, and slept my work. By a strange quirk of fate, I was sent to Utah for a few months to straighten out some legal hassles with a local environmental group. It struck me then what had happened to my life. What I had lost in my crazed pursuit for some frenzied and neurotic state of success. So"—he shrugged—"I asked for a transfer to the Salt Lake office."

"And if they hadn't given it to you?" Evelyn inserted.

"I would have quit. Evelyn, my life has been so much richer since I moved there eight years ago. Before that, I was just like you."

"Exactly what is that supposed to mean?" she stopped and turned toward him, her face now hard with irritation.

"I was riding on the same treadmill you are. I too felt trapped, not knowing how to get off, not even knowing that I wanted off. When I met you at that party last February, I was meeting a reflection of myself the way I used to be. Honey, believe me, you can get off."

"And just suppose that I don't want off? Suppose I happen to like my life the way it is? What makes you so sure I would ever want things to change?"

"It's that look in your eye that makes me so certain. That trapped-bird expression. Evelyn, I saw the change that came over you in Utah. Maybe you weren't as aware of it as I was. But you did change."

Evelyn's sigh had a hollow, desolate sound. She turned her gaze toward the street and watched the

Saturday joggers taking over the park. A group of young boys carrying a football crossed the path in front of them, their strides and laughter carefree and optimistic in the cold morning air.

"You've come a hell of a long way, honey," he whispered after he moved closer, his breath warm against her temple. "Don't stop now. Take those last few steps."

"I wouldn't even know where to begin, Michael," she said, her voice empty of emotion. "I've been riding this wheel for too long."

"Since your father left?" he asked gently.

She didn't answer, but crossed the street to walk the last block to the apartment.

"It's an escape, Evelyn. If you're using your work as fortification against hurt, then you're making a big mistake. The foundation won't hold. You need something stronger."

"And what might that be?" she quipped sarcastically as she kept up her brisk pace.

"You have to find a sense of peace within yourself first. Like I found in the mountains. And the second element you need in your life is love."

Evelyn closed her eyes briefly as a knifelike pain shot through her stomach. She would not listen to this anymore. She was going home, away from him, away from his sophist philosophies. She reopened her eyes, but her mind remained closed as she strode into the building and rode the arthritic elevator to the third floor.

Michael was beside her the entire way, but he knew she had closed him out. Damn, he had done it all wrong! He had sounded pompous and didactic, and had isolated her even further from him.

Evelyn unlocked her door and stepped across the threshold, turning to push the door closed. Its progress was blocked by Michael's arm and leg, braced against the doorjamb.

"Don't lock yourself inside, Evelyn."

"I always lock my door," she answered solemnly, knowing without a doubt that he had not been referring to the door.

"May I at least have a drink of water before I go?" He stepped in quickly, not knowing exactly what to do to keep from losing her, but realizing that something had to be done—and fast.

He closed his eyes briefly in a sigh of relief when he heard the door close—behind him.

"Help yourself," she muttered, walking off toward the bedroom. "I have to get cleaned up."

"Are you going in to work today?"

"Of course." She glanced around from the bedroom door.

"It's Saturday, you know."

She closed the bedroom door behind her without comment.

Michael shrugged his shoulders in frustration and went into the kitchen, pulling open several cabinets until he found one containing the glasses. Pulling one down from the shelf, he filled it with water at the sink, then leaned back against the counter and drank slowly.

Within moments, he heard the shower water running and his thoughts automatically drifted along the remembrance of her soft curves. He took a large gulp of water, then, staring down into the container of liquid, he fingered the glass indecisively in his hands. Finally, he placed the half-full glass of water down and pushed away from the counter.

Evelyn closed her eyes and let the warm spray wash over her body, easing away some of the tension in her muscles. She tried to shut off her mind to the image of Michael in her apartment. He was incongruous with its ambience, it being an image of refined, elegant silk, and he a symbol of an uncultivated, untamable earth.

Her eyes flew open like those of a surprised doe when the curtain was pulled aside and standing there before her was Michael, wild flames of desire burning into her flesh as his unhurried gaze ran the length of her body. Without understanding any of the reasons for it, Evelyn began to cry. She cupped her face in her hands and let the tears fall.

Removing his clothes as quickly as possible and never taking his eyes from her tear-streaked face, Michael stepped into the shower and wrapped her in his embrace, her damp eyes pressed against his throat as he soothed and caressed and murmured her name over and over.

He pulled her gently to him. "Why are you crying?" he whispered into her hair. She shook her head, unable to find the words to tell him what he did to her, physically, mentally, and emotionally. How he tore out from under her all the foundations upon which she had built her entire life.

He kissed the back of her neck where the warm water from the shower was hitting it, his tongue licking at the drops of moisture that accumulated on her skin. "Do you have any idea how much I need you?" he breathed.

She pulled back, tilting her head quizzically, and brushing away the tears on her cheek with the back of her hand. "Why?" she asked with wonder. "What... what have I ever given you that—"

"Evelyn." He touched her lips with his forefinger and smiled softly and enigmatically. "There's a feeling I get when I'm hiking through the mountains in springtime. It's a kind of"—he frowned as he searched for the right word—"challenge and... peace. I guess it's a mixture of the two."

He saw the confusion written all over her face and his mouth slanted sideways in consternation. His hands were cupping the sides of her head, his fingers massaging the wet, raven strands of hair. "It's sort of like when you're seeking something, the thrill of adrenaline that rushes through you as you're trying to find whatever it is you're looking for. And, at the same time, it's the sense of knowing instinctively that it's right there before you and has been all along. That's the feeling I get when I'm with you."

He pulled her closer, tasting the freshness of her wet face against his mouth.

She was too stunned to speak. She knew how much Michael loved the mountains. Even in the short time she had been with him there, she had seen his admiration for and oneness with the land. And she had wished often, during those seven days, that she could be the object of that much love and affection. Now, he was actually telling her that that was precisely the way he felt about her.

She clamped her fingers into his back, grasping the thick muscles that flexed under the warm spray of water. She didn't want to need this man, but despite her best intentions to forget him, she knew that she did need him. He was the only man—the only person ever—who had given her a feeling of worth within herself. It had nothing to do with how well she performed a job; it had to do with her. With what was inside.

As she leaned into Michael's strong body, she became aware of the subtle change in the movement of his hands and fingers. His palms glided down and, grasping her hips, fit her into the warm, wet contour of his body. The urgency of his mouth increased as it moved upward across her shoulder and neck toward her mouth. When his lips touched hers, she responded by opening her mouth and drawing his tongue into the dark recesses, her own hands moving across his damp flesh in intimate exploration.

The force of passion so long denied built up inside of Michael until he felt as if he would explode. Intertwining his fingers with hers, he pulled her hands upward to each side of her head, pressing her body against the shower wall.

Jolts of electricity shot through her body as his head lowered, and his mouth roamed possessively over her neck and chest and face. She closed her eyes and let herself be swept away by the feel of his mouth against her flesh and the sliding sensation of water running in rivulets between their bodies.

"Michael, I don't want to love you," she murmured as a last attempt to ward off his dominion over her.

He pulled his mouth away from her breast and looked up with half-closed eyes. "I know you don't, Evelyn. When you're on that treadmill, you lose perspective of what is really important in life. But nature has its hold on you, my love. On both of us," he breathed heavily. "Don't fight it, Evelyn. Nature always wins. Always."

Their mouths fused together in the intimate knowledge that there was a power much stronger than either of them, a force that ruled them both, that drew them inexorably together and would not release its hold.

He groaned softly as her fingers dug once again into his back, bringing him more urgently against her. Knowing she was powerless to resist the love that bound them together, Evelyn finally gave in to the raining shower of passion that enveloped them both.

When his fingers moved between her thighs, she shifted her body to take all the love that Michael Baylor could give her.

Chapter Ten

The room was still and dark, the color of the walls more apricot than peach in the low light. Turning her head slowly on the pillow, Evelyn read the clock on the bedside table, an anxious frown flitting briefly across her face. The blackout curtains, which hung behind the flowered drapes and darkened the room like night, belied the noon hour.

She knew she should get up immediately and dress, but she closed her eyes one more time, letting the memories of the morning enfold her for a few more minutes.

She shifted her head to the left and gazed at the man sleeping next to her. Michael's arm was thrown above his head, his face in peaceful repose, but his skin was shadowed by a scratchy half-day's growth of beard. Evelyn touched her chin and cheeks in remembrance of that face next to hers.

Michael had spent the morning proving to Evelyn over and over how much he loved her. She knew that now. His eyes, his touch, his mouth, his voice, all spoke of promises and love, and she had been swept into the power of that knowledge for the last four hours. Never had she known that making love could be as exhausting and exhilarating as it had been this morning.

It would be so easy if she could just disregard the fact that she already had a life here, a career that took everything she had to give and more. If she could just forget the promises she made to herself as a young girl and loosen her hold on those inflexible foundations, then she could freely express the love she felt for Michael. If only...

She sighed heavily and silently peeled back the blanket and sheet as she crawled from the bed. Tiptoeing across the room, she opened the closet and pulled out a gray wool skirt, white silk blouse, and black velvet blazer. She hung them on the doorknob of the closet, then moved on silently toward the bathroom. As she turned the doorknob to enter, his voice broke the surrealistic quiet.

"You're going to work," he stated in monotone. When she turned around, Michael had propped himself up on the pillow, his hands clasped behind his head. He was not smiling. He was watching her closely, a sense of the inevitable inscribed in his features.

"Yes," she answered after a long pause.

"I see." He expelled a long sigh and closed his eyes in thought.

Evelyn watched him for a moment longer, noticing the muscles tightening in his jaw. Then, she turned into the bathroom without another word and closed the door.

As soon as he heard the door close, Michael opened his eyes. He hadn't trusted himself to open them before now—not while she was standing there without clothes, without defenses. The anger inside of him had to be kept in tight rein and he'd been afraid of doing or saying something he would regret later.

He could hear the shower running, but this time he had no intention of joining her. She was going to work, going back to the sanctity of impersonal relationships. She was afraid.

"Damn!" He threw a bed pillow across the room where it hit the curtain, rustling it aside briefly to let a streak of sunlight shine in, before sliding down and settling on the floor without a sound.

After her shower, Evelyn dried her hair and wrapped it in a braided chignon at the back of her head. She applied just the right amount of makeup and slipped into her underclothes. She was trying desperately to think of anything but Michael lying out there on her bed. She had to get her mind where it belonged—on work. She had her own life to lead and Michael had his. He lived over two thousand miles away and she could not gear her life exclusively for those times when he would come back to New York on business and, perhaps, decide to look her up.

A teardrop glistened on her lower lid as she thought of all those miles between them. Wiping away the droplet, she finished dressing and forced her mind on problems at work.

When she came out of the bathroom, Michael was dressed and was sitting on the side of the bed putting on his shoes. They both stopped and stared at each other, the air charged with electricity between them. Evelyn was the first to move, bowing her head slightly and walking over to the closet to dress.

Michael finished tying his running shoes then stood, and deciding on the only course of action he could take, he walked over to her and placed both hands on her shoulders.

At the touch of his hands, Evelyn felt a debilitating weakness overtake her body. She leaned back against him and closed her eyes, smiling as his lips touched the top of her head.

He turned her around and looked down into her face, his eyes and mouth drawn with concern. "I'm going back to Utah tomorrow, Evelyn."

She looked away, directing her thoughts on a piece of lint that nestled in the carpet. Anything, she had to think of anything but the fact that he was leaving. She couldn't control the moistness behind her eyes and felt the pressure building. She wasn't going to cry! She wasn't! So he was leaving. She knew this moment would come. It was too good to last forever.

"I want you to come with me."

After all, his life was in Utah and he couldn't be expected to give everything up for—"What did you say?" She looked up with a start, her breath suspended in her lungs.

"I said I want you to come back to Utah with me . . . and marry me." Michael cupped her cheek in his hand. "I want you with me, Evelyn. We could make a good life there . . . together."

She was too shocked to answer, but her head had begun to move sideways.

"Evelyn, don't say no without even thinking about it," Michael admonished.

She stopped moving her head and looked at him, this time directly, with chin held high. "I'm going to lose you if I don't say yes, aren't I?" she asked with certainty already apparent in her moist eyes.

Michael shifted his feet and glanced down at the floor. "I have no intention of carrying on a once-every-six-months affair with you, if that's what you mean." He too was now looking directly into her eyes, wanting her to understand the depth—and the limit—of his feelings.

"And what on earth would I do in Utah, Michael? I'm meant to work." Evelyn's voice was tinged with frustration.

"So work if you want. I wouldn't expect or want you to sit around the house all day twiddling your thumbs."

Evelyn was shaking her head again. "Michael, I have built my life around this job. I'm in a great position with this company. How can I just leave it all behind me? It's very important to me."

"It's a crutch," Michael charged, his frustration and anger building by the moment. "It's the support you lean on so you won't have to give of yourself."

Evelyn's face hardened noticeably. "And you're asking me to lean on you—so what's the difference?" she yelled.

"God, you are thick!" he growled. "I don't want you to lean on me, Evelyn. I had people leaning on me in Vietnam—eighteen-year-old kids I commanded. And some of them died! I don't want anyone leaning on me. I want someone to stand beside me, to share her life with me. Damn, woman!" Michael raked his agitated fingers through his hair as he paced before her. "You have to be ready to stand alone, Evelyn. Maybe you aren't ready for that," he said, gazing intently at her for a long moment. "I—I thought you were but, well, maybe you're not."

"You're right there. I'm not strong enough to stand on my own where you're concerned. I need you too much, Michael. I'm afraid of that need. No...I'm terrified."

After snapping at the third person who walked into her office, Evelyn opened the drawer to take a couple of aspirin. It had been the most trying two hours she could remember.

When Michael had finally realized that she was not going to give him the answer he wanted to hear, he'd left her apartment to go get some of his own work done. But he had made her promise that she would meet him for dinner at Lloyd's tonight and that she would at least think about his offer. Think about it! As if she could think about anything else!

Michael wanted her to marry him and come to Utah. How simple and exciting it all sounded. But what if he too went through some sort of mid-life crises—just like her father—and decided that she was wrong for him? What then?

She had found a secure niche in this world and it was asking so much for her to give it up.

Evelyn swallowed the pills and drank a full glass of water.

"Now before you snap my head off," admonished Lloyd as he strolled into her office, "I just wanted to see if you were coming to dinner tonight."

Evelyn smiled sheepishly. "I'm not going to snap at you, Lloyd. And listen, about yesterday, I'm sorry..."

"Forget it." He waved his hand dismissively. "Hey, why don't you go home? It's Saturday."

"Well, why don't you?" she laughed.

"Oh, I'm only here to pick up something. I'm on my way to the golf course now." He walked over to the window, casually parting the blinds to look down at the street. He was silent for a few moments, gazing at something or nothing beyond the windowpane. "You know, Michael's like a son to me." He paused for so long that Evelyn thought he had forgotten what he was going to say. But he turned away from the blinds and looked down at her in her chair. "I'd like having you for a daughter."

Evelyn stared in mute silence as the burden of her decision crashed down upon her. "Lloyd, I don't know what to say...."

He patted her shoulder. "You don't need to say anything to me, Evelyn. To Michael . . . well, just say what's in your heart."

She watched him walk toward the door, then turn around one more time. "Will we see you tonight?"

She smiled weakly. "Yes."

"Good," he responded and left the office.

Good? Evelyn wondered. How good would he think it was when he found out what she would say to Michael? What she had to say.

"Have you seen it, Evelyn? No? Oh, you should. It's a great movie, and so funny."

Evelyn smiled, but felt the tightness in her own mouth. Vague bits and pieces of the conversation floated around her as she tried to keep her mind on the things that were being discussed. She was dimly aware of laughter and the tinkling of glasses and silverware as she sat at the large dining room table with Lloyd, his wife, and Michael. A live-in housekeeper traveled in and out of the room, bringing clean dishes for each course and removing the soiled.

It was the first time she could remember in a long time that she had eaten dinner with people who had things to talk about other than work. They were so carefree and jovial and she only wished that she could join the gaiety of it all. But her mind was trained on only one thing—how to tell Michael that she could not go with him and, even more than that, how to live with that decision.

Michael glanced down at Evelyn as she rearranged her food on the plate. He had been watching her closely all evening, waiting for a sign, a gesture, that would tell him what he wanted to hear. But she was so tense and quiet. Too quiet, he finally admitted with dismay.

As the dinner was coming to a close, their eyes met and locked—the flow of two separate lives crossing and intertwining, then each unraveling again to follow its own destiny—and both Evelyn and Michael knew what the answer was... what the answer had always been.

Chapter Eleven

"All I know is we lost the deal," one of the vice presidents grumbled. "Lost the whole damn project." He peered over his bifocals at Evelyn sitting so still and quiet across the conference table.

"What did happen, Evelyn?" asked another vice president, the one in charge of all South American operations.

Evelyn took a deep breath and looked around the table at the seven hostile faces that stared back at her. Only one out of the seven had even an ounce of sympathy for her. Lloyd stood out among the group of top corporate executives as her one ally. She was in big trouble. That much she knew. And, in truth, her alliance with Lloyd probably wouldn't help her much here.

In the last month, she had found it more and more difficult to concentrate on anything. She was dissatisfied, in a constant state of anxiety, and she continually botched up one project after another because of her lack of concentration. But this—this little fiasco topped them all.

She sipped at the glass of water in front of her. "It was a problem with the bid bond," she answered in a tight voice.

"What kind of problem?" came the chorus of voices from around the table.

"The problem is that she doesn't know what in the hell she's doing," Frank Groden snipped. "She should never have been put in charge of this project in the first place. She had no business—"

"That will do, Frank." Lloyd's voice rose above all others at the table. "I put Evelyn in charge of the land department three years ago and I have never regretted that decision. Now why don't we all let her explain, please."

Evelyn didn't look at Lloyd, but in her mind she was silently thanking him for his support.

"Well," she began. "As you know a bid bond was required. Our bank was to put up a guarantee with a Bolivian bank. If our deal was accepted by the Bolivian government but, for some reason, we failed to sign the contract, then the Bolivian oil company could draw down against the bid."

"Are you saying you didn't do the necessary paperwork?" one of the vice presidents asked.

"No. I did all that. I got the financial solvency statement by our bank. I had a set of financial statements notarized in New York and consularized by the Bolivian Consulate. I had the three letters of recommendation from previous clients. I had talked to the bank about the general terms of the bid, approximate percentage of the guarantee, approximate length of time for the bond. But I—I failed to give them the specifics."

"The effective date and the actual amount of the

bond, in other words," the agitated voices fired like cannons into her body.

Evelyn looked at each face around the table, feeling like a condemned woman before the firing squad. "I failed to give the bank the green light. I failed to instruct them to immediately send the tested telex to the Bolivian bank. On the day the bids were opened by the Bolivian oil company, the bank guarantee was not there."

The silence that filled the room was tangible. But Evelyn heard all the words that were not spoken, all the recriminations that were not verbally issued. Each one was like an ax that chipped and hacked away at her tottering pedestal.

As soon as the meeting was over, everyone gathered up their notepads and pens and headed back to their own office. Only Evelyn and Lloyd remained behind, and they were silent for several minutes after the room emptied.

"Thank you for your support, Lloyd." Evelyn stood and walked to the window and stared at her own reflection in the pane. What a mess she had made of things. Her job, her life … what a lousy, stinking mess. After a minute or two she walked back to the conference table, plopping down in the chair in weary defeat.

She looked at the glass of water in front of her and suddenly laughed. "Would you care for a drink, Evelyn? Yes, Evelyn, thank you, I believe I would. It's only water. Ah, well, the better to drown yourself with, right? Right." She picked up the glass and drained the water from it in one gulp.

Lloyd leaned his elbows on the table and watched her closely, disturbed by the gallows humor. It was so unlike her. "Evelyn, what's wrong?"

She shook her head. "I wish to hell I knew."

"Have you heard from Michael recently?"

Evelyn glanced up sharply, her entire cellular structure immediately activated by the sound of that name. "He has nothing to do with this," she hedged.

"You didn't answer my question though."

"No...I haven't heard from him since he left. Look, Lloyd, I know you thought there was something between us. Maybe you wanted there to be something, but—"

"He asks about you every time he calls, Evelyn."

Evelyn let her face fall into her hands. She didn't want to think about Michael right now. He was all she had thought about for the last month. When he left to go back to Utah, she felt as if something had died inside of her, rotting and turning rancid with each passing day. She could no longer concentrate on anything at work and her performance level had dropped substantially. Now, she had caused her company to lose an important project it desperately needed and wanted.

"He says there's lots of snow there now. It must be beautiful," Lloyd speculated, forcing her to talk about the one subject she most wanted to avoid. "He's going up to Expanding Horizons over Christmas to take a group into the mountains for a winter survival course."

Evelyn raised her head to look at Lloyd, no longer able to control the thrill she felt at hearing anything about Michael and what he was doing. "Isn't that dangerous? How do they keep warm?"

"I don't know," he shook his head in bemusement. "I can tell you one thing. You'll never in a million years catch me doing it. But you know Michael."

Yes, she knew Michael. Over the past month, in his absence, she had come to realize how well she knew him, how much alike the two of them were. Like alter egos, each living a half of the complete personality. Incomplete, that's what she was. Fragmented. "Where do they sleep?" she asked, trying to keep her questions light and politely interested.

"Apparently they build snow caves. Brrr! I don't really even like to think about it."

Silence permeated the room, more telling than any admission of love Evelyn could have verbalized.

"Lloyd, am I going to be fired?" she asked wearily, wanting to at least have one issue placed in perspective.

"No," he answered cautiously, weighing his words carefully. "But, Evelyn, I do think that you need to take some time off. I can see the pressure getting to you and..."

"You think I can't handle it, don't you? You think I don't have what it takes to—"

"I think," he almost yelled, then grimaced at his own outburst and softened his voice considerably, "I think that you have personal problems that are getting in the way of your professional judgment. I want you to take a couple of weeks off...for Christmas. Go away from the city. Why don't you go visit your mother? She doesn't live so far away."

Evelyn sat still, her hands in her lap and a sullen expression covering her face. He wasn't firing her, but this—leave of absence—was probably only a step away. Where would she go? Did she have the right to burden her mother with her problems—especially when she wasn't even in the Christmas spirit?

"She did ask me to come," Evelyn admitted reluctantly. "But I don't know. We never have connected too well."

"Why don't you go and give it a try?" Lloyd insisted. "You need the vacation."

He was right, she knew that. Not only was she not effective around the office, but she was obviously becoming an actual menace to the company's operations.

"All right," she smiled weakly, trying to muster some enthusiasm for the break. "I'll give it a try."

The Toyota that Evelyn borrowed from a friend for the holiday had a standard transmission. It took awhile to get used to the clutch and gear shift, but once she did the drive turned out to be quite enjoyable. As soon as she left the city behind her, the tension in Evelyn's body and mind lessened, many of her worries remaining back in the company's walnut-paneled boardrooms.

It was cold today, but the snow had been plowed to the sides of the highway in piles, and the six-hour drive turned into a pleasant diversion from her usual routine. The rhythmic glide of the wheels along the pavement served to iron out some of the emotional wrinkles inside Evelyn's mind.

By late afternoon, when she finally turned on to the familiar rutted road that led to her mother's house, the maple trees tall and stark against the red brick facade, she felt curiously enough like a wounded little girl returning to her nest for motherly comfort.

She stopped the car and got out slowly, hesitantly. She breathed deeply for courage, then walked along the narrow sidewalk and up the three steps to the porch. Opening the screen, she rang the doorbell.

As the weathered front door opened, Evelyn and her

mother stood awkwardly on opposite sides of the threshold for a long moment, each guarding the profound but complicated feelings between them, before they tentatively embraced.

Evelyn cleared her throat in embarrassment. "Hello, Mother. Thanks for letting me...come home."

"You know I always want you here. Whenever you want to come. Besides"—Mrs. Scott kissed her daughter's cheek with strained affection—"no one should be alone for Christmas."

Evelyn looked at her mother, at the features that reflected the genetic bond they shared, and she wondered silently about her statement. *You've spent many a Christmas alone, Mother. How painful has it been for you?*

They unloaded her suitcase from the car and Evelyn complimented her mother on the Christmas decorations. It reminded her of being a young girl, stringing the lights along the eaves. But she didn't say that to her mother. Those memories, the really good ones, were before her father left. A long, long time ago.

They walked back inside the house. "I hope you don't mind that I included you in a party invitation tonight, dear? I really couldn't say no." Mrs. Scott glanced at the grandfather clock that had been standing in the foyer for so many years, then looked back at Evelyn in apology. "It starts in an hour and a half."

Evelyn tried to hide her surprise, but it was there all the same. She'd had a vision all day of her mother sitting in the living room, waiting for her daughter to come for Christmas to give her life definition. But a party! Her mother was invited to a party.

As they carried her suitcase into the extra bedroom and unpacked Evelyn's clothes, they talked easily

about the insignificant things they had both been doing, about friends they shared in common, trivial dialogue that filled the house with voices but that did
nothing to bridge the gap between them.

"What kind of dress is it tonight?" Evelyn was already looking through her things and deciding that
nothing was appropriate.

"Oh, it's casual. Slacks and sweaters...whatever you
brought. The crowd I socialize with is very informal."

Crowd you socialize with? Evelyn was looking oddly at
her mother. She had assumed for so long that she
didn't have any friends, that she sat around the house
night after night pining away for a lost love. But a
crowd, she had said. Evelyn pondered the situation as
she put her things in the drawers. It suddenly seemed
that the world was moving on without her. Spinning
too fast for her to hold on.

The party that evening turned into four hours of
shock therapy for Evelyn. The woman who claimed to
be her mother was a complete stranger. She was carefree and happy and seemed well-liked among this
group of people. And she seemed to attract consider-
able attention from one man in particular, causing Evelyn to speculate about how close her relationship with
the man might be. Everyone was very friendly to Evelyn and she couldn't help but enjoy herself and feel that
she was welcome.

But once they returned home, the unspoken tension
between the two women had returned. It was not something that either could define. But it was definitely
there, and after a brief good night, they went their
separate ways.

The next morning, they both awakened early and

when Evelyn went down to the kitchen, Mrs. Scott was already heating a pot of tea on the stove.

"Good morning."

"Good morning, dear. Did you sleep all right?"

"Yes, fine." She was surprised at how well she really did sleep.

"If you need any blankets or anything, just let me know."

"Sure, okay."

Evelyn found the napkins and placed two on the table. She reached into the cupboard and brought down cups and saucers. The dialogue between the two women was off to its usual start—stiff and forced—and neither seemed able to bridge the gap that spanned between them. It had been this way for too many years. Evelyn had always blamed her mother for her father's desertion. Therefore, Evelyn's own vulnerability was the fault of her mother.

"You certainly seemed to have had a good time last night." Mrs. Scott looked up quickly and frowned. She had not missed the tone of annoyance in her daughter's voice.

"I had a wonderful time. I hope you liked my friends."

"Friends? Is that what William Talbot is—a friend?"

Mrs. Scott poured the tea and sat down across from Evelyn. "I have to admit, he's a little more than that."

The silence was tangible and Evelyn was aware in every passing moment how deep the chasm was between them. She didn't know her mother at all. And she was sure her mother didn't know her, either.

As she held the warm cup between her hands, she suddenly blurted out, "Are you going to let him desert you too?"

It was the first time the topic had ever been discussed between them and it stunned both women into ear-shattering silence. Her mother sat stock still, holding her cup in her hands, not bringing it any closer to her mouth.

In reality only a temporary lull had occurred in the conversation, but it seemed to Evelyn as if her question hung like a deadly insult in the air for eons.

"That's the way you see it, isn't it Evelyn?" Her mother spoke softly as she set the cup back on the table. "The way you've always seen it."

"How—how else should I see it?" Evelyn shrugged, furious with herself for even broaching the subject.

"You think of me as a weak woman. No, don't deny it, Evelyn. I know that...I've always known it. It's one of the things that has hung between us for so many years." Mrs. Scott tried to smile. "You're so strong and independent, so goal oriented and full of your own career-minded importance. And you think of me as weak and unmotivated and—"

"Listen, I'm sorry I brought it up," Evelyn bristled at the truth in her mother's statements.

"It needs to be talked about, Evelyn. You've thought it for so many years. Why not discuss it? Why not tell me what you really think, what you feel deep inside of you?"

Evelyn stared into her cup, then closed her eyes against the pain. She didn't want to talk about it. She just wanted the problem to go away. "I think I'm afraid," Evelyn admitted after a long moment's pause. "I guess I'm terrified of having history repeat itself."

"You mean with William Talbot and me?"

"No...with me."

Mrs. Scott was silent for a long moment, pondering the meaning behind her daughter's statement. "The sins of the father, so to speak?" Mrs. Scott offered.

Evelyn nodded her head. "Something like that."

Mrs. Scott took a sip of tea. "Well, all I can say, honey, is that you have to possess something before you can lose it."

"What do you mean?" Evelyn frowned at the cryptic remark and her inability to understand it.

"I mean, I don't think you need to worry about being deserted if you're not going to allow yourself to be loved."

"That's the problem." *Oh, Evelyn, shut up. Don't talk about it.* She looked up to see her mother's eyes narrowed on her.

"There's someone? A man?"

A lump began forming in Evelyn's throat and she felt a burning sensation behind her eyes. She wasn't going to cry, damn it! She cleared her throat to remove the blockage and opened her mouth to speak. But the words would not come. Instead, she began to cry, silent grieving tears that trembled upward from the base of her soul. She cupped her hands in front of her eyes. "Mother," she pleaded desperately, and Mrs. Scott immediately moved to her daughter's side and embraced her. She'd had lots of love tucked away inside her for so many years, and now her daughter was finally going to let her share it.

"I'm here, Evelyn," she crooned, as if she were holding and rocking her little girl once again.

"I'm so afraid," she said, raising her head to look at her mother. "There is a man...I love him very much. But I can't make a commitment to him. I'm afraid of admitting how I feel, because I might lose him...the way you lost Dad."

"In other words, you believe that never having that love at all is better than having it for a while and perhaps losing it."

"I don't want the same thing to happen to me that happened to you!"

"And what do you know about what happened to me, Evelyn?" Mrs. Scott held her daughter's face between her hands. "How do you know that what happened between your father and me wasn't the best possible thing?"

Evelyn stared at her mother with incredulous eyes. "But you were so distraught when he left you," she stammered. "I remember it clearly."

"Yes, I was distraught. I hated the fact that I was losing my husband, the father of my child, the only man I had ever loved. I think I even hated him for a while. I know I hated myself. For a long time, I took all the blame, letting it eat away at me as I wondered what I had done wrong. But I finally came to the realization that what was, was. There was nothing I could do about it. It was his fault as much as mine. I loved your father, but what was wrong with us would never have gotten any better if he had stayed. We would have ended up hating each other for sure. In my opinion, he left at just the right time."

"But I couldn't live with myself if Michael ever left me. I couldn't stand it."

"So you're going to deny yourself the opportunity to love him and deny him the opportunity to love you, just on the chance that he might leave you. Am I right?"

Evelyn sat back in her chair and wiped the tears from her face, still unwilling to admit that she had been wrong all these years. "In other words, you're saying it's better to have loved and lost and all that nonsense. Rather cliché, don't you think?"

"Cliché or not, Evelyn, it's true. And, if you deny yourself that chance, if you close the door to love, then I feel very sorry for you, Evelyn. No... I pity you."

The two weeks had passed, Christmas had come and gone, and she was now driving back to the city, solid, concrete manifestations that contrasted sharply with the unsettling vapor that now held Evelyn suspended in mid-air. All of the props had been knocked out from beneath her. Everything upon which she had based her ideas and her philosophies on life were now gone. Stolen from her in two weeks' worth of revelations.

Her mother had completely obliterated every notion Evelyn had had about her family life. Evelyn knew now that she had seen it all—her father's desertion and her mother's weakness—from the perspective of a child. She had felt the guilt and pain that any child feels when her parents divorce. And she had nurtured that pain, adding to it with her own limited knowledge of life, creating a world for herself so full of high-minded ideals and ceaseless activity that there was no room left for hurt. And no room left for love.

She had, at the age of thirteen, provoked a war that was not meant to be fought. And she had been fighting it ever since, entering one battleground after another without the faintest clue as to why she was there.

These past two weeks had been a turning point for her. A new beginning to her life. For the first time, she allowed herself to stop and think about tomorrow, about what her life would be like in five, ten, or fifteen years. She had taken these weeks to make some decisions and she would try to bring new direction to her life.

She knew that in her present state of mind, she was doing her company no good at all. She had lost her momentum and drive and the only right thing to do was to quit. She was sure Lloyd would understand, especially after she told him what she had to do.

She would go to Utah. She would talk to Michael. Maybe it wasn't too late. Perhaps he could help her learn to love and give of herself. She now knew that she did not want to live without him. She couldn't. She had been wrong from the beginning to deny her love for him, and she only prayed that it wasn't too late to tell him. Prayed that Michael would still love her enough to forgive her.

When she reached the outskirts of the city, the traffic swelled to jamming proportions. She shook her head in dismay. How could she have endured this hustle and bustle for so many years! She longed so for the quiet and peace of the mountains. She now understood exactly what Michael had been trying to tell her all along. That there's something more, a peace within yourself that you must find. She hoped she had found it this week, and that she had enough to give Michael in return for all he had given her.

She drove carefully through the streets, observing with detached interest as the throngs of people scurried down the sidewalks to their shops and offices. At least it was a weekday, and she would be able to talk to Lloyd right away. She wasn't even going to take the time to return her friend's car yet. She would do that after she talked to Lloyd at the office.

She parked in the company's underground lot, and hurried into the building, taking the elevator to the thirty-ninth floor. She distractedly greeted people that passed by her in the hallway, and continued to move with determined haste toward Lloyd's office.

Not waiting for the secretary to buzz him, she knocked on the door and entered. Holding the door open, she stopped and stared with bewilderment at the man behind the desk. The figure appeared only remotely related to the man she had known for eight years. His face was stark white and his eyes were glassy and red as he stared unseeing out the window. He was holding the telephone receiver in his hand and it moved toward its cradle in slow, precise motion.

"Lloyd! Are you all—Lloyd, what on earth is—" Evelyn felt the skin on the back of her neck drawing up and an ominous chill wound sinuously down her spine.

He looked up at her without recognition for several seconds. Finally, his large body sagged in the chair and his head began to move slowly from side to side.

"Evelyn." The one word seemed to expend all of his energy.

"What's the matter, Lloyd? What's happened?"

"It's Michael." He shook his head vigorously to jar his thoughts into a rational state, to grab hold of the disciplined mind that was used to dealing with crises on an everyday basis. "His company just called," he continued with more clarity as he tried to calm himself.

"What? What about Michael?" she almost screamed, impatient to know and, at the same time, wanting to shut it all out, to close her mind to what was happening.

"The group he took into the mountains..."

"Yes? What about them?"

"They were back at the school, packing up to go back to the city." Lloyd's head fell into his hands in utter weariness. "There was an avalanche."

Evelyn's breath stopped, clogging her throat with a lump of fear and pain so large and hard that she wondered if she would be able to breathe at all. "An avalanche?" she tried to speak, but her voice was nothing more than a choked whisper. "Michael? He's there... in the...?"

"The rescue party is already on its way," Lloyd answered, sensing the hysteria that was beginning to grip Evelyn, and knowing that he had to regain control of his own emotions. Someone had to remain calm, and even if it meant that he were losing the only son he had ever had, he would maintain a semblance of control.

Evelyn sank into the leather chair in front of his desk, her knees trembling and weak. She couldn't control the convulsive tremors that overtook her body, and she began to silently cry. She shed bitter, scalding tears for Michael, for herself, and for all those people who, like the two of them, had known a brief moment of love before it was lost forever.

Chapter Twelve

As the huge DC-10 eased its bulk down through the high cirrus clouds and made its final approach into the Salt Lake airport, Evelyn peered, with one last hopeful look, out her window at the sculptured, white summits of the Wasatch Range that lay to the east. She stared down into that vast expanse of endless snow as if she could actually see Michael in it and draw him away from the death grip it held on him, she alone rescuing him from whatever terror lay far beneath the shroud of snow.

She leaned her head against the seat back and closed her eyes, fatigue and worry lying in dark crescents above her cheekbones. She was only vaguely aware when the wheels touched down and when the jets reversed their flow, hissing and screaming down the runway until the plane finally slowed to a more earthly speed. In her mind, Evelyn could hear only her own guilt and terror and pain as she rewrote the script over and over again. It should have played differently. She should have come with Michael to Utah from the beginning. She should never have denied her love for him. She had been selfish, she had been blind. She had been a monumental fool!

If only it were not too late to change all of that. If only Michael could be found alive and they could play the final scenes the way they should be played—together.

If only, she prayed again. *Please.* It was all she had left. She no longer had her career to protect her from hurt; she had lost all of the foundations upon which she had structured her life. But she did have one thing left—hope. She would clutch that single emotion next to her for as long as she could because she knew that, in a few hours, that too might even be gone.

The airplane taxied up to the arrivals gate, and with mechanical movements Evelyn reached under her seat for her purse and flight bag. For the first time in her life, she had gone somewhere with only one small suitcase with which to carry her clothes. She had barely taken the time to even gather enough to fill it.

As soon as Lloyd had given her all the information about the accident, she had called the airlines for the next available flight. He assured her that he would take care of her apartment until she decided what she was going to do with it.

She felt a lump form in her throat as she remembered the lingering hope that flickered in Lloyd's eyes when she left his office.

Rising with the other passengers in the plane, she made her way up the aisle and into the expandable concourse. Before leaving New York, she had asked Lloyd to contact Michael's company to see if they would have a driver to meet her at the airport. As she scanned the interior waiting room, she noticed a middle-aged man walking briskly toward her.

"Evelyn Scott?"

"Yes." She nodded to the rugged, burly man who looked so ill at ease in these surroundings.

"I'm Martin Ingles from Impex," he spoke awkwardly, as if he were not at all accustomed to this type of mission. "I'm here to take you to the site." She noticed that he didn't call it a school. It was no longer that. Now, it was only a site.

"Thank you." She tried to smile. "I really appreciate your company having someone here for me. I could have rented a car, I suppose, but—"

"No, no, I'm happy to help. And...I'm real sorry about what's happened."

"Have you heard any more news?" she asked worriedly as they headed down the long hallway.

"Not much, but—say, do you have any luggage?"

"No." She held up her flight bag. "This is it."

"Good." He took the bag from her and they continued walking through the main lobby. "I don't know too much that's happening right now. I heard earlier that they found a couple of people, but I don't know if they were alive or not. They're just damn lucky that the owner of Expanding Horizons was driving up to the school when it happened. He saw it all and was able to radio the forecast center."

"Forecast center?"

"Yeah, the Forest Service has an avalanche forecast center here in the Wasatch. It's one of four in the West."

Martin opened the door and she followed him through the parking lot, trying to loosen the tight knots of dread that were constricting her chest. The air sweeping down off the mountains was cold, but the sky was now clear and boundlessly blue. "At least the weather won't hamper the rescue operation," Martin's remark was an optimistic spark that contrasted sharply with her own waning flame of hope.

He led her to a red Blazer and after opening the passenger door for her, and climbing behind the wheel, he backed the vehicle out of the parking lot and headed through the streets of the city, circling Temple Square and driving on east toward Immigration Canyon.

There had been little conversation between them, and for that Evelyn was grateful. She needed time to think. They would be there in less than thirty minutes and she needed to prepare herself for what they might find. A torn image of Michael's lifeless snow-covered body flashed before her mind and she was unable to control the shiver that rattled within her body.

"I'm sorry," Martin misinterpreted the action. "Let me turn on the heat for you. I'm so used to this cold that I don't think much about it."

"I'm fine, really," she tried to smile. "Do you work with—with Michael?" Her voice split along a thin crack of air. She cleared her throat and tried to blink away the tears that blocked her vision. "I'm sorry. This is rather ... difficult for me."

"I know," he smiled sympathetically. "But everything that can be done for them is being done. This rescue team is the best in the business." After a moment's pause, he continued. "No, I don't work with Michael, but I've met him. I'm a manager for some of the mining operations. I work on the sites rather than in the office."

Evelyn glanced over at the man behind the wheel. His large, muscular arms and weathered skin accurately reflected his many years of physical labor in harsh climates.

"How did you two meet?" He looked over at her with curiosity. "I mean, you being from New York and all."

"We met at a party last February and then I went through a session at Expanding Horizons last summer."

"Yeah?" His eyes widened with a mixture of awe and disbelief as he glanced once again at the chic woman beside him.

Evelyn turned to stare out her window at the passing scenery. As far as the eye could see from the windows of the Blazer, the snow lay everywhere, blanketing the mountain peaks and wrapping the evergreen trees in pyramid-shaped packages. The aspen, whose shimmering leaves rustled and quaked in warmer air, were now stark and still, their naked branches merging with the white backdrop.

Conversation was again suspended as Martin concentrated on his driving. He had shifted the Blazer into four-wheel drive, gearing the transmission for the icy upward climb. The road serpentined and slanted ever higher, the deep-grooved treads of the tires digging tenaciously into the road to keep the vehicle from swerving off into the piles of snow at the side of the highway.

Evelyn saw the roadblock ahead at the same time Martin slowed the truck, and she felt a wave of dismay attack her midsection. They weren't going to let them through. She had come all this way and they weren't going to let her go to Michael.

Martin stopped and rolled down his window to talk to the flagman in an orange nylon parka.

"Sorry, this road's closed. Avalanche ahead," he said between frozen lips.

"Yes we know." Martin growled. "We've been called in to help. Jim McGrath sent for us."

The man glanced through the window at Evelyn and looked skeptical.

"She's a relative of one of the victims," Martin offered.

"Well, I ain't supposed to let no one through. But if you say—what'd you say that guy's name was?"

"McGrath. Jim McGrath."

"Haven't heard the name," the man frowned, scratching his chin.

"He's in charge of the project, you idiot," Martin yelled with indignation. "Now get out of my way, before I have you reported for obstructing a rescue operation."

When the man stepped back and waved them on, Evelyn realized that she had been holding her breath since they first stopped.

"I hope to hell he doesn't check to see who Jim McGrath is," Martin muttered.

"Why? Who is he?"

"My car mechanic."

"You mean he has nothing to do with the rescue operation?" she asked incredulously.

"Nope. Not a damn thing."

Martin turned the car off the main road, forcing the vehicle to follow the snow-narrowed trail that wound upward into the mountains and toward the school.

Trucks and jeeps and helicopters blocked the entrance into the camp, so Martin pulled the Blazer off the trail into the packed snow, parking it between two pine trees.

They had to walk several hundred feet through knee-deep snow to get into the camp and Evelyn was glad she had worn her fleece-lined boots and corduroy pants for warmth, but her calves and ankles ached from the unaccustomed exercise.

As they entered the campground, Evelyn's first impression was one of shock, followed by a heavy numbness. Most of the buildings were gone, but a few walls still stood, tilting under the enormous weight of the snow. Only one wall of the main lodge seemed to have been spared from the rushing tide of powder that swept down in a devastating flood from the mountains. Even the cabin where she had spent that first night with Dorothy Miller was gone, broken and washed away by the force of the snow.

To Evelyn, it seemed as though nothing but chaos reigned in the campground. There were at least a hundred people milling about doing absolutely nothing.

"Why aren't they doing something!" she cried, panic pushing her through the crowd to get things organized.

Martin took her elbow and held her back. "They are, Evelyn. They are. See that line of people over there?" He pointed to a string of about twenty volunteers standing in a row, walking slowly across the snow carrying metal poles. "Those are telescopic rods that can reach way down in the snow."

She shuddered as she watched those rods plunging into the white mounds, imagining the tip of one hitting against Michael's body. "Rather primitive," she mumbled.

"It is, but it works."

"What are those dogs doing?" she asked anxiously, pointing to the huge black furry animals that plodded heavily across the snow, straining against the leashes that held them.

"Those Newfoundlands are trained to sniff out bodies in avalanches. If the rods don't find them, the dogs will."

At that moment, a stretcher carried by four men moved toward them. "Out of the way!" they yelled at anyone in their path, including Evelyn and Martin. They stepped aside, but she craned her neck to see who was lying on the canvas frame. A young blond-headed man, with blood and ice caked in his beard, shook violently upon the stretcher, and Evelyn noticed that his skin was blue and crystalized in several spots.

"Is he going to be okay?" Evelyn clutched onto Martin's arm in fright.

Martin looked grave. "Don't know. At least he's alive."

The men with the stretcher moved on through the crowd and lifted the canvas board into the waiting helicopter. Immediately the chopping whirr of the blades filled the air, and white powder swirled in funnels around the crowd, stinging their faces with the loose, flying snow. Evelyn shielded her eyes as she watched the helicopter lift off the ground, hovering for only a couple of seconds before it took off over the trees and toward the city.

Martin held onto Evelyn's elbow and steered their way through the crowd. As he reached a young man with an orange Ski Patrol band on the sleeve of his jacket, he stopped. "How does it look?" Martin asked worriedly.

"Pretty good luck so far," the young man said between directives issued to other patrol members. "We've found four. They were trapped inside the main lodge, behind that masonry wall." His mind seemed to be trained on something Evelyn and Martin could not see. "It's like they knew it was coming," he said in a daze before once again becoming all business. "That's the only thing that saved them."

"What about the others?" Martin asked. "Weren't there twelve in all?"

The young man looked pensive for a moment. "We've found two others." He shook his head and Evelyn had to clench her teeth to keep from screaming. "Hey, get that dog over there!" The young man grew distracted and hurried away to make sure his orders were being carried out.

Evelyn scanned the crowd and noticed a reporter standing within a cluster of spectators. He was speaking into his microphone and the television camera was trained on his every gesture. As they wound their way through the milling crowd, she could just make out a few of the words he was saying. "The scene is now under control . . . dedicated young men and women . . . through the long hours of morning . . . in the cold." Another man was now standing next to the reporter and was answering the rapid-fire questions that were directed at him. Evelyn could only discern bits and pieces of their discussion. " . . . being used for?" the reporter asked as he pointed to the large canvas tent that had been erected on the site. The other man looked tired and drawn as he nodded his head, and Evelyn strained to hear what he was saying. "Yes . . . building gone . . . place to warm up . . . use as morgue . . ."

Evelyn's frantic gaze jumped to the tent. A morgue? Did he say they were using that tent as a morgue? Pressure began to build inside her stomach, a nauseous surge billowing upward through her chest. She leaned dizzily toward Martin and he carefully led her to a large boulder where she was able to sit and let the sickness ease back down into her stomach.

"They found him because of his transceiver," someone was saying to a group of people only a few feet away from Evelyn.

"Who's that?" another voice joined the discussion.

"The instructor from the school."

Evelyn's heart seemed to stop as she listened intently to the conversation.

"Yeah, it was switched to 'receive' and they just followed the tone. That's how they found him."

"How did he look?" an eager spectator wanted to know.

"I don't know. They carried him into the tent, that's all I know."

They carried him into the tent. They carried Michael into the makeshift room they were using as a morgue! Evelyn's gaze swept across the devastation, landing on the line of people systematically plunging their telescopic rods into the snow. A flash of red hair in the line caught her attention and she realized it was Josh, Michael's best friend. His face was grim as if he had seen all the horror he could take in one day. Suddenly, she knew. His face was telling her what she had been denying for an hour. She knew. And, all at once the people and the noise and confusion and press coverage and fear became too much for her to bear. Martin was standing in front of her, looking around the camp for something constructive to do and Evelyn could no longer keep the tears from falling. Great heaving sobs racked her body as she realized all she had lost, and she began to shake violently all over. A hand touched her shoulder and someone else helped her stand and ushered her through the crowd toward the tent. Everything in the periphery of her vision had turned black and her ears were ringing with painful vibrations. Through the fog of her mind, she was aware that people were making way for her. A relative, the voices seemed to say. Take her to the tent, another ordered.

No! Not there! She was dimly aware that she was fighting the arms that held her. She didn't want to go to the tent. *Not to the morgue!* Without much of a struggle, they were able to get her through the opening and seated on a chair against one canvas wall. Someone stuck a steaming mug of coffee in her hands, but she was too shaky to hold it, so it was removed. She heard a deep, angry voice intruding its way into her mind, a large figure pushing through the crowd of people around her, and she felt an incredible warmth as someone wrapped his arms and a blanket around her.

She leaned into a broad, hard chest and heard her name whispered over and over.

"Evelyn." Cool lips touched her temple and she instinctively lifted her face toward the source of that soothing voice. She stared, uncomprehending, unable to believe that the face before her was anything more than an apparition of hopeful madness.

"Michael?" His skin was pale and his hair hung in wet strands where ice and snow had melted in it. A small bruise on his right cheek was slightly puffy and turning purple. The blanket was wrapped around his shoulders and his hands and lips were cold and light blue.

He pulled her head back against his chest and expelled a long, torn breath. "Evelyn, my God, what are you doing here?"

She began crying again, but this time they were tears of weary relief and happiness. She wrapped her arms around his waist and held him tightly against her while the tears fell.

"I thought you were...they said this was being used as a...I was so frightened for you, Michael. For me." Evelyn wiped the wetness from her cheeks with the back of her hand.

"It's okay, everything's all right now." He stroked the back of her head with his hand and then wiped away the moisture from his own eyes.

A man walked over to them and reluctantly interrupted, telling Michael that they needed him outside immediately.

Michael raised from his squatting position, looked down at Evelyn and smiled gently. "I'll be back as soon as I can. You'll be all right here?"

"Yes, I'll be fine," she sighed and leaned back into the chair, giving her eyes and her mind a few minutes of peaceful rest. After a little while, she had calmed her nerves sufficiently to rouse herself from the chair and see if she could be of some service. Three women and a young boy were making sandwiches on top of a wooden door that was propped across two chairs, and they were delighted that she offered to help. A continuous stream of rescue crew members and anxious relatives filtered in and out of the tent all day, looking for sustenance and a few minutes' respite from the cold.

With a renewed sense of energy, Evelyn volunteered for any job that needed to be done. She saw very little of Michael other than at a distance. His services were needed to help find the remaining victims of the avalanche. Two more had been found by two o'clock and only four more remained. The ones not seriously injured, including Michael, had been treated for minor injuries inside the tent and were now helping with the rescue operations.

Once, when he came in for a bite to eat, he pulled her aside, wrapping his arms tightly around her waist. "How did you know, Evelyn?"

"Lloyd told me. He's very worried, Michael."

"We'll call him later. Evelyn . . ." He sighed, running his cool lips across her cheek and into the hair above her ear. "Thank you for coming. It means so much to me." He gazed down into her eyes, a tender expression that said more than words ever could.

Before she could tell him that she had done it for both of them, they were interrupted by a reporter and his camera crew.

"Ron Simpson, Channel Six News. Mind if we ask you a few questions?" The camera was already rolling as if the question were merely a rhetorical one.

Evelyn glanced at Michael and noticed a wariness she had never seen in him before. His eyes held a hopeless, lost look, and she wondered if he was going to hold up under the strain.

"You are the instructor who was in the avalanche with the eleven victims, is that correct?"

"Yes." Evelyn kept her arm around his waist, buffering him against the storm.

"What were the events leading up to the disaster?"

"We had been camping for a week back in the Unitas. There had been a lot of hard snow for the last couple of days, high winds, drifts. Unstable masses all over the mountains. We were heading back to the camp and had planned to sleep out one more night. But— God, I don't even know when—yesterday I guess it was, I felt a shifting in the snow. It was settling under our feet. A funny kind of *woomp*. I thought we should get back to Base as quickly as possible and leave for town. It just wasn't quick enough."

Dead silence filled the air for a moment and Evelyn glanced anxiously at Michael's distraught face. He was blinking his eyes, trying to hold back the tears and he had to clear his throat several times before he could continue.

"Being behind that masonry wall of the lodge is what saved you, isn't it?"

"Yes."

"Why were some of you in the lodge and some not?" The reporter continued the questions as unemotionally as if he were covering a city council meeting.

"Jamison, Roberts, Ellingston, and I were storing some equipment. The—the others were—God!" He turned his back on the camera, but not before the emotional pain and self-recriminations had been revealed to everyone who would watch the evening news.

By seven o'clock, all of the victims had been found and a lethargic gloom had settled over the crowd. The victory of finding four people alive this morning had long since evaporated as the day of grim reality wore on.

Michael had been helping with the rescue attempt all

afternoon and now he was seated in a folding chair in-side the tent. Evelyn stood beside him and watched the director of the school approach. When he reached them, he placed his hand on Michael's shoulder.

"You did everything you could, Michael. No one could have done anything more."

Michael looked at the director but didn't respond. What was the point? The people were dead and he had been responsible for their safety. He had done every-thing he could and yet they hadn't lived.

"Why don't you take him home?" the director was saying to Evelyn and she nodded in response. She looked down at Michael with the question in her eyes. Did he want her to come home with him?

"What about the families?" Michael didn't look at Evelyn, but at the director instead.

"I'll notify the victims' families, Michael. You just let your lady take you home and get some rest."

Michael finally looked at Evelyn and the question that had been in her own eyes was now reflected in his. Their eyes locked in a mutual embrace, answering the needs in both of them. His slow smile struck every nerve in her body, moving beneath her flesh like a sen-sual caress.

He reached up and stroked her cheek in awe. It was too good to be true. Evelyn here in Utah with him. All day he had resisted the impulse to drown in her pres-ence, to let her enfold him and drive away this mad-ness. "Let's go home," he whispered.

Home. Home with Michael. He still wanted her with him. And it was where she had always wanted to be. Though she had tried for months to deny the existence of her need for him, it had always been there, waiting, expanding, filling up her life until nothing else held any significance in comparison.

She smiled down at him. "Yes. Let's go home."

They met up with Josh and asked him to give them a lift to Michael's cabin down the canyon. As he explained to Evelyn, "My car I'm afraid was pulverized by the snow."

As they loaded up in Josh's Cherokee Chief, Evelyn took one last look at the school. Its crumbling ruins resembled the devastated center of a war zone, left as only a shell of its former self. She was sad to see it end this way.

The drive back down Immigration Canyon was a quiet one, all three of the passengers in the truck too tired to even discuss the events of the day. Josh turned onto another thin trail, hardly wide enough for a car, and drove about a quarter of a mile. There in a small clearing, with a snow-covered stream behind, sat a tiny, buff-colored stucco cabin, its roof flat except for the chimney protruding from its surface.

The jeep pulled to a stop and everyone sat silent for a long moment. Josh turned to Michael and the two of them clasped hands in a bond of unspoken communication found only between men who together have survived the best and the worst that life has to offer.

"Good-bye, Evelyn." Josh finally turned to her and kissed her on the forehead.

"Thank you, Josh. For everything."

Michael helped Evelyn out and carried her bag as they walked to the front door. Stepping up on a small stone porch, Michael stomped his boots out of habit to remove the snow before entering.

Evelyn glanced around the porch and front yard with

a sense of wonder. So this was where Michael lived. How often she had tried to imagine him in his own house. She hadn't even known whether to picture him in a house or a snow cave or a tepee!

She touched the impervious stucco exterior and smiled to herself. It fit him, she decided. And it fit her.

Michael opened the door and waited for her to clean her own boots and enter.

"Your door wasn't locked!" Evelyn looked startled, as though something or someone might be waiting for them on the other side of the door.

Michael's grin was lopsided, but still an encouraging sign that he was making the transition from the tragedy on the mountain to home. "This is Utah, honey, not Manhattan."

"But what if someone wanted to steal your things?"

"You haven't seen my place yet, Evelyn. Believe me, what I have, no one would want."

Evelyn stomped her boots the way Michael had and followed him into the house. The door entered onto the kitchen, a cozy room with a stone floor and tiled countertops. A butcher block table butted up against one wall and a large earthenware pot next to the door held a rifle.

"I thought you said it was safe around here." Her voice had a tiny quake in it when she saw the gun.

"It is." Michael was sitting in a kitchen chair, slowly removing his boots and grimacing with pain.

Evelyn walked over and knelt down in front of him to help pull them off. He closed his eyes in gratitude and leaned his head against the wall, letting her take care of him.

"Then why the gun?" she asked, unable to get her

mind off the ominous threat of it perched so menac-
ingly by the door.

"Animals," he replied without opening his eyes.

"Oh." Animals. She swallowed hard. Of course.
That explains it. She finished removing his boots, then
walked over to the door and promptly slid the bolt lock
closed.

Michael opened his eyes and smiled crookedly. It
would take some time for her to get used to mountain
ways, he knew. He was watching Evelyn as she moved
about the house, tentative steps as if she were afraid to
touch anything. He wanted more than anything for her
to like it, to feel at home here, to want to stay. When
she walked into the living room, he rose stiffly to follow her.

The kitchen was connected to a small living room. A
round, stone fireplace dominated the far wall and
served as heat for both this room and the one beyond.
Navajo rugs were scattered across the wooden floor and
a tweed couch was the only large piece of furniture in
the room. Evelyn took note of every detail in the
house—the sand paintings on the walls, the Indian bas-
kets and pottery that lined the mantel, the stereo equipment and books that filled several shelves.

Unaware that Michael was behind her, watching her,
she stepped through the doorway to the bedroom. Her
gaze centered on the queen-size brass bed that filled
the small room. A thick down quilt was thrown haphazardly, yet invitingly, over the sheets. On the floor were
more Indian rugs, and a large Colombian tapestry hung
on the wall at the head of the bed. The fireplace was
open on the bedroom side also, and she felt a warm
tingling sensation slide along her nerves as she thought

of lying in that bed with Michael, the two of them watching the fire in the afterglow of love.

That bed. She couldn't seem to tear her eyes away from it and she almost jumped when Michael slid his arms around her from behind. Did he know what she had been thinking? Did he have any idea what she wanted?

"I know it's not very large, Evelyn. But we can add on." His voice was slow, but she detected a fluttering note of hope in it and she turned to look at him. He pulled an Indian print curtain aside, revealing a large porcelain bathtub, perched on four claw feet, and smiled when he saw her pleased reaction. "The closet is small," he hurried on, pulling open the door to show her. "But I own five acres here, so there's plenty of room for expansion. You'll need room for your clothes, and we'll want—"

Evelyn stepped up to Michael and stood on her tip-toes, pulling his mouth down to meet hers. "Shut up," she whispered before pressing her lips gently against his. "I love it."

They stood this way for several seconds, her palms pressed against his cheeks, their eyes locked in silent communication.

"The house?"

"Everything," she murmured. "You."

Michael pulled back, holding her at arm's length while he deciphered the truth in her eyes. "You mean that, don't you?"

"I've never meant anything more in my life, Michael. I've been in a self-destruct mode for so long, slowly dying over these last few months. Suicide is what it's been."

Michael closed his eyes and pulled her close, burying his mouth in her hair. "Then let me heal you, Evelyn. Let's heal each other."

She reached up and gently touched the swelling on his cheek, and said a prayer of thanks that he was alive. "I've never been in any real physical danger. Were you terribly afraid, Michael?"

"I've been afraid before," he answered solemnly. "But yeah, I was. And you want to know what scared me the most, what really terrified me?"

She nodded slowly, running her fingers through his now dry, but matted hair.

"I was terrified that I would never see you again. Nothing else in those hours seemed important to me, Evelyn. Dying itself was nothing compared with that." He held her tight and groaned against her face. "God, I'm glad you're here! I'm here. We're alive. Please tell me you'll stay."

"I'll stay, Michael. I promise, I'll stay."

"I'll make the house as big as you want it. Or we can move into town. I'll make it good for you."

"All I want is you, Michael. I don't care if it's in a lean-to at twelve thousand feet. Together we'll make it good. I love you."

Michael cupped her face in his hands and smiled down at her, tenderly, lovingly. His gaze shifted to the bed, then back to her face. "Let me build a fire," he spoke softly.

"No." Evelyn placed her palm on his chest. "You rest. I'll build it."

Michael watched her for a moment with fascination, then nodded in assent. "The logs are on the porch." He smiled as he dropped wearily onto the bed, too tired to think about removing his clothes.

"I'm going to call Lloyd first and tell him you're okay," Evelyn said as she went into the kitchen, placed the call to Lloyd and, after leaving the message on his recording device, slipped her boots back on and unlocked the door to the porch. She had to make several trips back and forth from the woodpile to the bedroom, but eventually she had enough logs to start a nice fire. Some newspaper was stacked on the floor in the corner, so she wadded up several pieces and stuffed them under the logs. Pulling a long match from its clay container on the mantel, she struck it on the inside of the fireplace and lit the paper.

Within minutes, a roaring blaze filled the fireplace and the small room was suffused with its renewing warmth.

Next, she turned on the faucet in the bathtub, filling it with very warm water. She removed her boots, then sat on the bed with Michael and stroked his head and face and neck with gentle fingers.

His eyes were open, watching her, absorbing her presence and her touch. Her black hair was pulling loose from the clip that held it in one long strand at the back of her head. Reaching up, he unfastened the clasp and pulled her hair forward, arranging it over one shoulder with his fingers.

Her hands moved to the front of his shirt and slowly began unfastening the buttons. As the shirt fell open, her hand slid across the solid expanse of his chest, warming his still cold flesh with her own.

When the tub was almost full, she got off the bed to turn it off. When she turned around again, Michael was lifting himself off the bed to finish undressing.

"Here, let me help you." She eased the shirt from his arms, then rested her hand on his belt buckle.

"What made you change your mind, Evelyn?" he whispered. "What made you come here?" He helped her unfasten the belt and slide the zipper down on his jeans.

"It was so many things, Michael. It was you and Lloyd and my mother and learning that I could exist without my career." She looked at him with a sheepish glint in her eyes.

He smiled back. "I told you the wilderness experience would change your life."

"You changed my life," she countered seriously. "You made me see that I was worth something as a person. You're the best friend I've ever had."

"I hope to God I'm more than that." Michael pulled her head against his chest and she kissed the weathered skin that still smelled of pine and snow and clean mountain air.

"You are, Michael. You are everything to me."

They held each other for a long time, relishing the feel and closeness of each other. Finally Michael let her loose and he removed the rest of his clothes, and with Evelyn's help, stepped into the tub, easing his body down into the warm water.

His eyes closed with fatigue, so she moistened a washcloth and began rubbing it across his chest and shoulders.

His hand covered hers, stopping its progress across his skin. "You come in too."

"Are you sure?"

"Positive."

She smiled and stood, removing her own clothes as quickly as her tired body would allow.

Climbing into the tub, Michael made room for her

by shifting his legs. She sat cross-legged, facing him and once again picked up the warm washcloth and smoothed it across his skin.

His hand lifted to cup her breast, then slide down her side.

"What did Lloyd say about you coming out here?"

"Well, he was so worried about you, Michael, that I'm not sure he really understood that I was quitting."

"He's losing a good employee."

"I'm sure I'm replaceable." She shrugged and grinned when he looked at her. "I told you I've changed."

"Don't change too much, lady. I kind of like you the way you are."

"Kind of?"

He reached out and pulled her head down to meet his mouth. "More than kind of." His lips closed over hers gently and lovingly. When he pulled back, he studied her seriously. "I really am glad you're here. I'm not sure I could have weathered all of this alone. All that's...happened."

Moments of silence slipped by while the tragedy of lost lives filled the air around them. A light snowfall had begun again and wet flakes slapped against the windowpane, its quiet rhythm tapping only the periphery of their minds. Inside the cabin, they were safe and warm. The yellow glow from the firelight added a flush to the cream-colored walls, flickering and casting warm shadows that trembled around the room. The ripples of water that moved around them reflected the golden glow of the flames.

"Tomorrow I want to go see the families. But, hell, I don't even know what to say to them." He leaned his head back against the rim of the tub and sighed.

"It's not your fault, Michael."

"No?"

"No." Evelyn clasped her hands around his neck, pulling his face close to hers. "No, Michael."

She scooped up some water in the palm of her hand and wet his hair, then shampooed and rinsed it with cups of warm water. His eyes were closed as she massaged his head and neck and shoulders to relieve the tension in his muscles.

"Michael, I want you to know that I'll learn to climb and rappel and tie bowlines and..."

"That doesn't matter, Evelyn."

"It does matter. It matters to me."

Michael finally smiled. "Honey, a girl scout you're not."

"Oh, yeah?" Evelyn's eyes were narrowed to tiny slits. "We'll see about that."

"Okay, we'll see." Michael's hand stroked her jaw and his fingers moved back into her hair, letting the long, dark strands sift through his fingertips. He stood, pulling her with him, and stepped out of the tub. He wrapped a large bath towel around her shoulders and pulled her next to him, their moist bodies touching intimately for the first time in over a month. And tonight it stirred the love between them, forming a bond that would hold them together through anything, even through the pain of this day. Nature had wreaked havoc with Michael's physical and emotional being. But together, they would see it through. Evelyn had found her strength, an inner resource that could never be conquered. And she knew she would have to draw upon it to help Michael with the memories of this tragedy.

As she dried with the towel, she watched Michael

turn down the bed. She smiled. "You know, I realize now that the bargain I made with you the first night at Expanding Horizons was more like a plea. I wanted you so badly, and it was the only way I knew to have you."

She crawled in between the sheets beside Michael and let him pull the heavy down quilt up over them. He pulled her into his arms, her head resting on his chest. "No more wars, Evelyn. No more bargains or battles or skirmishes or defeats. Just the two of us working things out together."

"Yes." Evelyn pressed her lips against his chest, then rested her cheek once again on him. "I love you, Michael Baylor." Her hand slid slowly down the warm solid wall of his body, resting against his side. "I always will."

"And I'll always love you, Evelyn."

Within minutes, their eyes had closed on the harsh reality of the day, and wrapped in each other's arms, they surrendered to the peaceful bliss of sleep and to the triumph and victory of a love that could not be defeated.